SCORPION

James R. Poyner

For Princess,
For over twenty years,
A wonderful model of devotion,
Who will <u>always</u> be alive...
In my heart.

National Library of Canada Cataloguing in Publication Data

Poyner, James R., 1950-
    Scorpion

ISBN 1-55369-026-5

    I. Title.

PS3616.O96S36 2002   813'.6   C2001-903427-X

TRAFFORD

This book was published *on-demand* in cooperation with Trafford Publishing. On-demand publishing is a unique process and service of making a book available for retail sale to the public taking advantage of on-demand manufacturing and Internet marketing.**On-demand publishing** includes promotions, retail sales, manufacturing, order fulfilment, accounting and collecting royalties on behalf of the author.

Suite 6E, 2333 Government St., Victoria, B.C. V8T 4P4, CANADA
Phone   250-383-6864   Toll-free   1-888-232-4444 (Canada & US)
Fax   250-383-6804   E-mail   sales@trafford.com
Website   www.trafford.com
TRAFFORD PUBLISHING IS A DIVISION OF TRAFFORD HOLDINGS LTD.
Trafford Catalogue #01-0428   www.trafford.com/robots/01-0428.html

10   9   8   7   6   5   4   3   2

Chapter I

A SUMMER'S DAY

IT WAS A wonderfully blue summer's day in seventeen seventy-seven, with the sea air and the light spray, tossed over the bow, refreshing to face and soul. That blessing of good weather, of course, made it the sort of day that brings out the best in all of us, particularly those whose profession is traversing the seas, great rivers and broad lakes of the world. Yet, regardless of our life's course, sailor or not, we all shine with happiness, and find our daily tasks infinitely easier, when the weather is just right. At least, those of us with good hearts and minds do.

Unfortunately, not all good hearts are brave enough to shine and carry out their arduous tasks amid the darkest of times, nor are all good minds clever enough to challenge the wily servants of evil. Both may try, and bless them for that! The men of *Scorpion*, however, *were* brave enough to meet such tasks and foes because our loyalty to each other—*and* to our infant nation!—was absolute. We had the heart and the steel to stand up to villains, or at least, to challenge those who would deny us our freedoms. That was part of our calling, as well. After all, a good storm of Nature, Who is by no means evil, can challenge a sailor, just as surely as any storm brought on by other humans. We were ever ready to stand up to either, and so, we plied the water as resolutely as the tide climbs the shore. To my mind, there was nothing that could deter us from that course.

We would follow it. We would live or die by what we found along the way. We would accept, without apprehension, the tests of man and Nature. Fill our sails, then, and away! Roll on!—roll on!

The ocean off Boston seemed far-removed from the main war, far-removed from the chatter of infantry muskets and the boom of field pieces, but then that war, the one for American independence, was characterized by many side-shows. *Scorpion*'s part was the same as that of the several other barks that were armed with two-dozen twelve-pounders. We were to harass enemy shipping, while endeavoring to avoid traps, since we could ill-afford to lose even one ship.

As a privateer, we patrolled the shipping lanes, took prizes, and usually escorted those ships to Boston, where they and their cargo were sold to help finance the war. Our operations demanded that we be both brave and clever. Further, the British, who were by no means servants of evil, were, first of all, our enemy, and more, they did not lack for good minds to lead them in military affairs. What's more, they were intent on denying us the independence, the liberty, we had declared, and that was enough for most of us.

Another thing my crew and myself had to exhibit, in order to succeed with our mission, was strength. We had to be able to endure all the physical hardships associated with running a ship: furling and unfurling sails, turning the windlass to lower or weigh the anchor, working the pumps to counteract a leak, pulling at the oars of a long boat linked by cable to the bow of the ship when *Scorpion* was becalmed, and a myriad of other strenuous activities. Oh, now and then someone would complain that a task was hard, but never would he refuse to complete it, not even if he was asked to get down on his hands and knees and scrub *all* of the main deck. He would *try* to complete the task, and that often was enough for me. The willingness to try meant that man was still a dedicated part of the ship and crew. What more can a Captain want?

To the man, we each recognized the importance of performing our tasks without fail, no matter how insignificant or menial they seemed. To not carry out a job meant letting down the entire crew, and that was not the sort of failure that a responsible, caring man wanted to have attached to his name. No, we each had our duties, and we each fulfilled them, no matter how much they taxed our strengths. Yet, by working together, our strengths became combined, and so, the tasks were made easier.

Then, in addition to our physical duties, there were the many parts that had to be played out each time we went into action. Again, strength was called upon, along with a goodly amount of energy. Once we went into general quarters, cannon balls, kegs of powder and the like had to be brought on deck, and then they had to be distributed to the gun crews. For each of the latter, handling their piece meant employing a good amount of strength and energy, while using both with a proper degree of accuracy and efficiency that translated into speed.

A harness of rope and pulleys, called a block and tackle, was bound to each cannon. The device moved the gun in and out of its port, in much the way a stable hoist was used to raise sacks of feed up to the loft. For each cannon on *Scorpion*, two or more men tugged at the ropes threaded through the pulleys. First, the gun was pulled back, a swab laden with water was shoved down the muzzle to clean the inside of the barrel, wiping out any lingering sparks in the process, then powder and a 12-inch iron ball were run down to the breech and tamped in place, and finally the cannon was wheeled back into its port and aimed.

Then at the command, *Fire!*—a long match was set to the breech hole, and seconds later, the cannon boomed out its ball and recoiled. Again, the piece was pulled back, swabbed, reloaded and returned to its firing position. A good gun crew could be set to fire again in five minutes, the time it takes to *twice* swing a ship a hundred and eighty degrees, or to turn two broadsides. *Scorpion* had the agility to make such a pair of pivots in four minutes, and her gun crews never failed to be ready. Then, on those occasions when it was impossible to turn the ship, usually because of a countercurrent or wind, the number of men on the harness was doubled, while other members of the idle gun crews stood ready to assist in anyway they could.

Aye, there was a lot of physical exertion that went into working each piece, and with two-dozen cannon, that meant that a lot of men had to be employed to fight a battle. Still more would be aloft, and at least one would be at the helm. Not surprisingly, the gun deck could become very chaotic during a fight, and all sense of order and duty could be lost...*unless* the crew was well trained and disciplined.

For the British Navy of that time, discipline meant breaking a man's spirit so that he became no more than a dumb animal capable of being taught to perform certain duties—without question *and* without failure! For the young American Navy, discipline was much milder. We did not want to break our men. Instead, we wanted them to be alert and quick thinking because we were convinced that that would ultimately give us the edge. So, we trained them as best we could, and when a man needed to be punished for a minor offense, punishment would be in the form of a constructive task, such as white washing the top of the mainmast.

It was then that the man's willingness to try became a factor. More serious matters usually meant court martial, demotion, or even time in the brig. That my crew worked as well as it did was a testament to the effectiveness of our form of discipline. That none had ever been found guilty of serious infractions was a further testament. Yet, I believe it was still more important that we gave our men and ourselves a sense of pride in both what we were doing and in our ships. My men and I were quite proud of our nation and its hope for freedom and equality, but we were especially proud of our charge.

Scorpion was a stout, but fast, three-master with a white stripe through the gun ports, the rest of the hull being a weathered black. Typically, for a bark, her first two masts were square-rigged, with the third, the mizzen, also square-rigged but with the lower sail running fore-and-aft. Otherwise, the main deck was one smooth expanse that was unmarred by a raised forecastle or quarterdeck. Aye, she was a fast, modern ship for her day! Spirited and agile, she responded with a wonderful quickness to her helm, and while she groaned and creaked like any ship in bad weather, there was a marvelous buoyancy in her roll and other actions that made it a joy to take her wheel in any sea and under any circumstance.

We were as confident in our ship as we were in ourselves. What better union could there have been! How important that was...and still is!

"Sail, ho!" Tibbs cried from the forward nest.

As I clung to a line near the mainmast, I looked up at my long-time shipmate with fondness and asked, "How many and where away?"

"Three ships, sir! Four points to starboard! Wait!—smoke!—gunfire!"

The dull booms reached my ears moments later, and I commanded, "General quarters, Mr. Jenkins!"

"Aye, sir!" the First Mate returned.

With that, he stepped over to the foremast and rang the brass bell that hung a few feet above the deck on that spar. It sounded clear and loud, a fair herald to the human thunder we might soon produce. In response to that clanging, men surged out of the various hatches. A few rigged the hoist that would bring munitions up to the main desk, others sprang to their assigned guns and started preparing them for a possible conflict, while still others carried muskets and munitions-laden pouches aloft. After an appreciative shoulder clap of Seaman Dickens, Tibbs took his weapon, a pouch of shot and a horn of powder from the other lad. Moments later, his musket primed, he resumed his watch duties in the nest.

"Stand by with our colors, Mr. Newton!"

"Aye, sir!" the Second Mate replied and directed two men to be ready to hoist our national banner off the mizzen.

"Keep us advised, Tibbs!" I called to my old mate.

"Aye, sir!"

Now since we were the only American warship in the area, the fighting on our horizon was for us to investigate. It could be a French raider attacking British merchantmen bound for New York, or a British man-of-war firing on Dutch ships trying to smuggle goods into Boston to supply the Continental Army through that port. Whatever the case, we were under orders to discover the truth and lend assistance where it was needed. Yet, our orders had never anticipated what we were to find.

Unfurling every available sheet of canvas, *Scorpion* seemed to bloom like a flower of Spring as it plied toward the scene in question. As always, I wanted us to respond by reaching the site of trouble as quickly as possible. That was implied in our orders from Boston.

What we found that day gave that hope for speed a new reason.

✳✳✳

MOMENTS LATER, TIBBS called, "Sir!—it's a *pirate!* Seems to have gotten the better of a British brig with designs on the merchantman that the Brit was escorting! Aye, they're swinging about to board the merchantman!"

"Understood, Tibbs!" Knowing the possibly savage fate that awaited both of the pirate's victims, I added, "All guns, standby!"

"Standing by, sir!" the chiefs of the gun crews replied, sharp and loud, nearly as one.

"Mr. Newton, raise the colors!"

"Aye, sir!" the Second Mate crisply answered.

My crew responded with a wonderful efficiency to my newest orders, and by the time the embattled sails first appeared on the horizon, we were ready for action. That also meant having a dozen men standing by with primed muskets in the nests, and with Tibbs as their formal leader. Further, Lieutenant Newton had taken the helm. All three mates had been carefully schooled on how best to maneuver the ship in a fight. The rest of the time, the crewmen took turns at the helm, just as they did on the mastheads, except the foremast, which was Tibbs's daily assignment—he was my *best* pair of eyes, both in ability and experience.

So, by my commands, handsome Lieutenant Newton, whose blond hair ended in a fashionable queue, took us on a course that would bring *Scorpion* up on the pirate's exposed side. *Graywolf*, like *HMS Bennett*, was a two-masted, square-sailed brig, and both carried eighteen twelve-pounders, nine per side, with three-pound swivel guns on either side of their bows. They were, of course, utter contrasts: one was the pride of a highly civilized nation, the other was filled with ruthless rogues; one stood for beliefs and virtue, the other stood for greed and the vilest villainy; one was the defender of innocents and crowns, the other cared for neither; one was an appendage of what some thought was a bully king, the other was unquestionably nothing more than a bully. If the infant United States ever hoped to take her proper place among the nations of the world, then she had to take a stand against pirates, even when that stand benefited ships of the nation that was trying to deny the United States her independence, and even when that nation thought privateers like *Scorpion* were little better than pirates.

And so, we rushed headlong into the fray, down the watery rise toward the trough of danger.

✳✳✳

BY THE TIME we swung into position, *HMS Bennett* had already lost the top half of her foremast and was unable to prevent the pirates from boarding the equally helpless merchantman. Our turn brought us to within a few hundred yards of *Graywolf*. Its lines, spars, guns, and crew were all clearly visible, but the latter seemed unaware of us. They should have been more curious about the looks of hopeful amazement exhibited by those on the British ships.

"Port guns!—fire!" I cried.

Nearly as one, the chiefs of the twelve guns set their matches to the fuses in the breech holes. Seconds waxed and waned as everyone stood clear, ears covered, and then the entire ship shuddered as all twelve guns went off, briefly enveloping us in white smoke. The dozen projectiles barely arched at that range as they rushed through the air and smashed into the pirate. One ball landed a glancing blow on her mainmast that opened a noticeable crack from deck to royal yard, another fell on one of their cannon, smashing its carriage and leaving its barrel twisted and useless. Other rounds left a dozen of the rogues dead or wounded, wrecked one of their boats, and ruined their windlass.

Graywolf answered with but three of her starboard guns. They did little damage, because of the pirates' panicky haste, and because they fired when our pivoting turn had exposed only our bow to their cannon. Yet, before we could finish swinging around to deliver our starboard broadside, the black-flagged brig had withdrawn her boarding party from the merchantman and was pulling away.

Realizing that part of *Seacastle* and her innocents were now exposed to our guns, I stayed my command to fire, while Mr. Newton brought us around for another try at the fleeing ship. We took it, shot up a few more lines and put a hole in her stern just above and to starboard of the rudder. She made no effort to respond, and I let her go. We had foiled her intent, and that was enough for me.

Further, *Graywolf* had left two crippled ships in her wake, and I felt it my duty as a seaman and a gentleman to make certain they were not in danger of sinking before I did anything else. At the same time, I did not wish to be forced to engage the British warship when we already had more of an advantage over it than had *Graywolf*. We not only had more cannon, we also had all of our abilities, which could have let us dance around *Bennett*, if we chose. So I had us maneuvered until *Seacastle* was between us, before I hailed the Captain of the merchantman from our port rail.

Captain Marble responded, by coming to his starboard side and saying through his trumpet, "Thank you for your assistance, Captain Dawes! We are in your debt! I have signaled *Bennett* to keep her distance! What's the nearest port? We have some wounded! Need repairs!"

"Boston is ten miles due west!"

I was about to offer them escort, especially since we could not claim either ship as a prize, when one of the Captain's officers rushed up to him. Captain Marble's face paled at the news from his junior. That paling announced trouble as surely as a boom of thunder. It alerted me to the danger of rough seas on the human stage. It *urged* me to be ready.

Of course, it was hard to tell from that distance what the nature of the trouble was. Had I somehow known before hearing an explanation, I am convinced I would have done nothing differently— even if I had known *all* that would transpire. No, *Scorpion* existed to take certain chances, and what we were about to experience was one of them. As for what the ill wind had brought, I could only guess that we had not driven away all of *Seacastle's* dark fortune.

Finally, Captain Marble turned to me and explained, "Sir, my First Mate reports that those devils made off with one of our passengers, Miss Deborah Walton, a niece of *Lord Cornwallis!* Can you help?"

To some, it might have been a difficult question to answer. For me, the right thing seemed to be what my beliefs urged. In short, I could not turn away from a plea for help, even if it came from my enemy. If that is not a tenet under what we call humane behavior, then perhaps, it ought to be. Certainly, many of our religions preach such a thing, although those of us who are good-hearted should already know that.

"We will do all that we can, Captain, and when we have succeeded, we will bring her to Boston—God willing!" I answered.

"Then may He watch over you, your crew, *and Scorpion!*" Captain Marble said. "Surely, *Scorpion* is not the blight some claim!"

"Thank you, Captain! Now, when you get to Boston ask for Captain Turnwick and tell him *all* that happened here, and that I, Captain Sam Dawes, do *not* consider either of you a prize!" I replied.

"I will do as much!"

I touched my hat and then gave orders for us to pursue *Graywolf*.

⌘⌘⌘

Chapter II

A BEGINNING

WHILE IT TAKES people strong in heart, mind and body to crew a ship, and to make that ship a successful venture, we must not forget that a ship is but a macrocosm of a person. One, who is strong in all three human aspects—the physical, the spiritual, and the mental—as Plato suggests, will be a success in life, just as surely as a ship manned like *Scorpion* will succeed in its mission. Of course, the same philosophy can be expanded to include an entire nation, perhaps even the world as a unified entity. Indeed, we are only limited by our drive and our imagination, and by how much we are willing to work together.

Naturally, the larger the entity, the harder it is to achieve such an ideal balance of the human elements. Yet, if each individual within that group has achieved such balance, then it goes without saying, that that entity, no matter how large, will be balanced, while through that balance, the individual will *want* to work with others. At the same time, the nature of a person's position in the crew—or society—will determine which of the three aspects that person primarily provides to support the whole. Yet, if that person is strong in all three aspects, then he or she will be ready to contribute effort in all three as the need arises. Certainly, if a man on a ship is taught to use his reason, as well as his strength, he not only will arrive at a better solution for a problem, he will also use that reason to discover ways to become more efficient with his normal regimen of tasks.

Scorpion, both ship and crew, is a model of all of that. The ship herself must be balanced if she hopes to remain afloat in the roughest seas. Too much tilt either way during a storm will almost surely doom her and all of us. Yet, like the best of corks, she bobs upright, again and again. She has a good roll to her.

On the other hand, her crew enjoys a balance, because each officer and man is encouraged to lead a balanced existence. Reading and games like Chess among the men are encouraged and practiced to further their minds, while my officers and I routinely take time to repair the various small boats. Then, each Sunday, a worship service is held on the main deck for the entire crew, while meals are always initiated with a word of thanks to the Maker.

Aye, balance *is* there in the ship and crew, and by now, you should to begin to see that balance, through strength in all three aspects, does not mean equal portions of each. Instead, *Scorpion's* balance is furthered by our devotion to each other and our mission. Yet, we also have regular work parties, each led by an officer who is encouraged to physically help his party achieve its goal. Through that, not only does the officer lead by example, but also we achieve teamwork, and you are about to see where ours was sorely tested by circumstance.

The pirate took us on a course that was generally due south. I guessed she was headed for the Bahamas, where she hoped to find refuge, while she made repairs and discovered a way to profit from her captive. My plan was to let *Graywolf* take us where she would, and to make sure she never got far beyond that port. How we would recover Miss Walton was something I was not ready to consider. There were too many intangibles to do anything other than let events follow their natural course. Sometimes you *must* let that happen, while watching steadfastly for your opportunity to act—just be *ready* to act! So we went on, and while initially we never gained on them, we never lost ground either. In fact, I was always able to see the tops of *Graywolf*'s sails while standing to one side of the bow.

That was true even when day was replaced by night, for the moon was full that evening, and the brig's silhouette was an easy thing to discern.

✳✳✳

THE SEA, AT night, is a wondrous thing, especially when the sky is clear, as it was that first night. The great multitude of stars and the ivory gleam of the moon fill one's chest with awe. They also serve to remind a good-hearted viewer that there are greater things than the self. How can anyone look up at such a display and still have no regard for a Maker? How can anyone consider all that we humans are, and then propose that we are merely an *accident* of fate? No, I say you must have *faith* in other things, or you are apt to end up conceited, cold-hearted and cantankerous—a veritable pirate—a sad end, indeed!

So, I tarried on deck for some while, enjoying the fresh, moist smells of the salt water, the musical creaking of the ship, and the quiet hum of several men singing as they stood near the bow. As always, I made a point of visiting that group. In the Royal Navy, such fraternizing would be looked on with horror. This, however, was the fledgling *American* Navy, founded to serve a nation of free men. In theory, there were no classes or other divisions. In practice, there was evidence that both were beginning to disappear. There was, in fact, an emerging sense of balance and harmony in our new society, and from that viewpoint, *Scorpion* was a microcosm. So I welcomed our departure from the strictures that could easily have marred the start of my career with George III's Navy.

From the beginning, thanks to my father, I saw no point in mistreating men or officers in the name of discipline and the King, and I saw no harm in making direct contact with the men and developing a cohesiveness based on compassion and understanding that would achieve harmony, balance's elusive partner. It was radical thinking for the era, but then, so was declaring our independence from Britain. That first night of our chase, I went forward and quietly listened to the tune of the lads standing to port of the bow, one of our swivel guns just beyond them.

"You lads may be in the wrong profession," I judged at the song's end, making them all look my way with rapt attention.

✳✳✳

THEY WERE USED to my watching them by then, and so, they no longer felt compelled to stop their song when I first appeared. What was more, Tibbs was among them, and by then, they all knew the special regard we held for each other. Yet, they also knew that I was a disciple of our old master, which made them comfortable through their proper understanding of me, even when Tibbs was not among them.

"Certainly, if there is ever a call for a seamen's choir, I shall gladly recommend you."

"Thank you, sir," Tibbs said with a smile, as the others nodded.

His eyesight was impeccable, and so, he had long been permanently posted to the crow's nest atop the foremast. Indeed, it was that trait of his that was at the base of our regard. As for that, I believe it is fair to say that we enjoyed a friendship. Tibbs, you see, was one who was afraid to offend by being impolite, so he was *always* polite to me, while on the other hand, he was still delighted to find me being just as polite toward him, which is one way of saying that we respected each other. Yet, I felt that each of us would gladly give his life for the other, and in that way, we were also friends. Then there was the unmistakable—if unspoken—mutual fondness for each other, which added depth to our consideration for each other.

"So, Captain, do you think we can get a rolling deck under our feet when we sing in concert?" he asked.

We laughed again, and I added, "Well, you certainly bring a warmth to the ship with your song. We'll likely need that warmth to fall back on when we go up against *Graywolf*. Another broadside would've gotten her today, lads!"

"Aye, sir!" several of them sang.

"Still, you did well with the ones we gave her. That's what frightens an enemy far more than size or might—a foe who delivers a precise, devastating blow and then quickly readies the next. You lads have again displayed that quick precision—our record as a raider demonstrates that, and you ably demonstrated it today— my compliments!"

"Thank you, sir," Tibbs said as the others echoed him. "We'll get *Graywolf* soon enough and save the lass, too—God willing!"

"God willing!" the others chorused as I nodded.

Then my old shipmate added, "Remember, sir, it was He what got us where we are *and* put us in league with the Rebels, sure enough."

"No doubt, Tibbs. I also remember how He brought you and me together."

For a moment, the fore deck was silent, as we all dwelt in the past, a past that all of those there shared with Tibbs and me.

⌘ ⌘ ⌘

Chapter III

A FEW MEMORIES

PORTSMOUTH WAS TEEMING with ships of every size and description that fair, but chill, morning late in 1771. Laden with four tiers of guns, there were towering men-of-war, the great champions of the sea for the nation that ruled the waves, the battleships of their day. Frigates, which had two decks of guns that could land a powerful blow, were more common as the British Navy turned toward smaller, faster, more agile ships. Of course, merchantmen were everywhere, cycling through the routine of docking, unloading, loading and setting sail. Others waited for their turn to tie up at a dock, while their masters anxiously hoped that their cargo wouldn't spoil in the meantime. It always amazed me that an island nation of modest size could achieve such greatness. Perhaps, though, that greatness became, in turn, the root of its downfall, or was it the unflinching devotion to division?

Still, Portsmouth was the port of empire and commerce—the best example of England's place in the world. Indeed, the vast array of vessels filled me with pride as I stood looking over the scene. By then, the hired coach had pulled away, and left me with my thoughts, my feelings and my modest sea chest. I was, at last, on my own. I was, finally, set on the path to my fortune. Where it would take me was a vague image on the horizon—an image of serving God, King and country from a rolling deck. Certainly, at times, I had dreamt, or wondered, if there shouldn't be more. Something within, if not from my father's liberal teachings, suggested that, indeed, there was more, but I had yet to realize what that was. Perhaps, that more was tied up with my fate.

"Marvelous sight, eh, sir?" a burly, young man asked as he stopped at my side and rested his white duffel bag at his feet.

Our uniforms clearly identified us as officer and man, just as surely as our different forms of luggage did. Yet, we enjoyed several bonds, and I have always preferred to strengthen the latter, rather than stress our differences to the point of driving a permanent wedge between us. Father had urged all of us to prefer the former—that was part of his teachings. Among other things, he stressed that the noted wedge was not only inhumane, but also contrary to the emerging philosophy of the Age of Enlightenment. Men had to learn to put aside their differences, he urged, and then he ventured to add that the time was coming when we would have to view women as equals, as well. It was foolish to consider half of the human population as only capable of bearing and raising children. That was wasteful and inefficient thinking. No, we had to learn to manage better if we hoped to maintain our dominion of the world. The wedges had to disappear.

Smiling at the sailor, I agreed, "Marvelous, yes, but also an unforgettable image to go with the start of my first voyage with His Majesty's Navy. Is this your first, as well?"

"Aye, sir. I'm shipping on *HMS Breeze*. I heard Captain Whyte was a good and fair master, and I wanted to do my first voyage with just such a man. In return, I offer keen eyesight and a willingness to work hard."

"I'll keep that in mind since that's my ship, as well," I noted. "I'm Sam Dawes, Lieutenant, Junior Grade."

"Seaman John Tibbs, sir," he answered and saluted.

I beamed and returned the salute. Tibbs had a wonderful glow about his person that suggested his enthusiasm for his new venture. I knew from Father that such zeal would produce a good worker who would devote himself to the tasks at hand, and who would willingly help others as the need arose. His passion could also be contagious, especially if his superiors, in the presence of other individuals, encouraged it.

Then, offering him my hand, I said, "Well met, Tibbs." When his look questioned the gesture, I added, "It's all right, my father has taught me to greet all men in this way. They do it in America, not only as a gesture of peace and friendship, but also to help erode the artificial divisions placed on society. Like Father, I want to *erase* those divisions."

"Then well met, Lieutenant Dawes!" he agreed and shook my hand.

✳✳✳

WITH THAT, WE shouldered our pieces of luggage and made our way to the ship. *Breeze* was a newly commissioned bark, armed with twenty-four 12-pounders and a pair of three-pound swivel guns, and she was in need of a purposeful shakedown cruise. Ours promised to be that since we would take a handful of young gentlemen to Calcutta where they would act as staff for the Royal Governor. From there, we were bound for America to serve as an armed mail packet at the request of Deputy Postmaster Benjamin Franklin.

"Permission to come aboard, sir?" I asked and saluted First Mate Lieutenant Webster as he sat at a small table that held the crew list.

"Name?" he replied blandly without returning my salute or looking up.

"Lieutenant Sam Dawes, and this is Seaman John Tibbs."

"Is he dumb?" Webster cried, looking at me with a scowl.

"Not I, sir," Tibbs answered. "The Lieutenant was merely being courteous, sir."

"Is that so?" Webster returned, reddening another degree or two. "Well, *both* of you should understand...*Each* man—*and officer!*—shall answer for *himself* aboard *this* vessel! Is that clear, *Lieutenant?*"

"Yes, sir!" I replied.

"Good! In the future, I trust you will also remember that it is improper for an officer to befriend a seaman...to say *nothing* of shaking his hand!" the First Mate added with indignation as his face reddened still more.

William Webster was ever quick to anger, especially with those inferior to himself. He had little patience for those same people, but only a tad more for his superiors. The latter he hoped to push aside with the least excuse as he sought to maintain, and promote, his divisive philosophy. For First Lieutenant Webster that belief, as he vowed, was absolutely correct.

"As for you, *Tibbs*," he continued, "you are to also remember that unless an officer gives you permission to speak freely, you are to keep your opinions to yourself."

"Mr. Webster," an older man said as he stepped over to the table from his post near the mainmast, a naturally white queue adding contrast to his black tri-corner hat.

"Yes, Captain Whyte," the Mate replied, without standing or looking back at the man.

"Who are these fine young men?"

"Lieutenant Dawes and Seaman Tibbs, sir," the Mate answered mechanically.

We saluted the Captain, he returned the gesture, and then he enthused, "Welcome aboard, Mr. Dawes! Welcome, Tibbs!"

"Thank you, sir," I said, offering him my hand.

Webster frowned at that. He knew it was a symbol of defiance for his views, but said nothing when the Captain promptly shook my hand. That our master then grasped Tibbs's hand utterly horrified the First Mate. Tibbs was, of course, as amazed as he was honored. As for me, that action of Captain Whyte was wonderful to behold. It reaffirmed what my father had taught me, while it also served to signal what the tone of the voyage would be like. Of course, I did also wonder if my father, who had gotten me the assignment, somehow knew the Captain, or knew of him.

"So, Lieutenant, since you apparently know Tibbs here, where would you have me post him?" the Captain wondered.

"Crow's nest on the foremast, sir. Keen eyesight, like Tibbs's, shouldn't be wasted."

"Indeed not, lad, " the white-haired man said, beaming.

It was already apparent that he liked me. I was his sort of officer, or so, it seemed. At least, we *appeared* to share the same philosophy on respect and regard for others. I also sensed that, like myself, he wanted to make sure of those appearances. It is no good to go about assuming such things. Better to address them at the start than set yourself up for a bad surprise, such as an angry rebuff. Better to learn how things truly stand at your earliest convenience than falsely build on your assumptions.

"Please, note that by Tibbs's name, Mr. Webster. You have signed them in, haven't you, man?"

"Hadn't a chance, sir," the Lieutenant admitted, somewhat fearfully because he loathed even the hint of a lapse on his part.

"He was distracted by your coming to greet us, sir," I readily explained.

Webster didn't know what to make of my providing an alibi for him. I then signed in and urged Tibbs to do the same, which further removed Webster from rebuke. To some gentlemen, in those days, a rebuke was the worse sort of punishment—sterner than any number of lashes, with a longer lasting effect. It was even more debilitating when it came from someone that person regarded as a poor superior, which was William Webster's view of Amos Whyte. Of course, in my opinion, Lieutenant Webster's views on the merits of our master were as distorted and ill founded as those he had on the relations of officers and men. Yet, I always had the good sense, and the proper discretion, to keep my views to myself, unless I was asked to reveal them by a superior for purposes that would favor either the ship, her crew, or her mission.

"Well, this is a fine looking ship, Captain," I observed with a smile as I looked aloft.

"Thank you, Lieutenant. Report to my cabin once you've secured your bunk."

"Aye, sir."

"Tibbs, after you've claimed your place, I'd like you to come back on deck and watch for our passengers, *five* young gentlemen. They'll likely need a hand with their belongings."

"Aye, sir!" Tibbs returned, saluted, and moved off smartly for the forecastle, but not before he had noted with a wink in an aside, "Thanks, for the mention about me eyesight, Lieutenant Dawes."

"My pleasure, Tibbs."

"Bart!" the Captain then called.

"Aye, sir!" a young lad responded and ran up to us.

"This is the Third Mate, Lieutenant Dawes. Lieutenant, the cabin boy Bart Winston," our master explained.

"Hello, Bart, keeping everything shipshape?" I asked as I held out my hand.

With a happy grin, the spunky chap of a dozen years, shook my hand and enthused, "Oh, yes, sir!—Lieutenant Dawes!"

"Well done!" I said and smiled as Webster moaned again at my brazen familiarity.

The Captain, however, directed, "Bart, my lad, see Lieutenant Dawes to the surgeon's cabin. They'll bunk together."

"Aye, sir! This way, Lieutenant," the boy urged, as he shouldered my sea chest.

"Right behind you, Bart!" I returned.

✳✳✳

IF THERE *ARE* treacherous waters to beware of in the human experience, they are those associated with communication between individuals. When we fail to communicate well, or at all, those waters are apt to become rough, to the extreme of isolating us. How easily can you reach an island that is ever encircled by heavy seas? How well can you perform a task when you did not hear all of the instructions because your mind was focused on something else? How often do you wonder why no one seems to listen to you?

Yet, at the base of communications is respect and understanding. If you do not properly regard another person, how will you react to what that person tells you—how well will you listen? Further, if you have trouble getting along with another individual, is it possible that that is due, in part, to not understanding each other? Well, it only follows, that such difficulties are magnified manyfold when the individuals must dwell in close proximity for a fair amount of time. The men and officers of a ship must necessarily live in such conditions. Captain Amos Whyte knew that as well as any. To him, good communications among shipmates, and especially between Captain and crew, were paramount to the success of the voyage and, more importantly, to the success of the ship.

As we tarried in the cabin I was to share with Dr. Greenwald, Bart said, "I'm not sure who I like more, sir, you or the Captain."

"Well, I'm honored that I even come close to the Captain in your estimation, lad. Still, do you think it really matters which of us you like more? Isn't it better to find that you like *both* of us?"

"Aye, I suppose it is, Lieutenant! Certainly, it'll be a much more pleasant voyage having *both* of you on board," the cabin boy said and grinned sagely.

"Well, now you've got the right idea," I noted, while telling myself that Bart himself would help to make our venture agreeable. "I think you'll find Tibbs to be a friend, as well. He's a good, dutiful sort. You don't need to discipline him to make him a good sailor. You just need to show him what needs to be done, and then you stand back and let him do it."

"Tibbs, hey?—the man you recommended for the forward nest?"

"The same," I said as I finished stowing my things in the vicinity of the unclaimed bunk. "Well, there, that's done. Now show me to the Captain."

"This way, sir," Bart said, waving for me to follow.

So, per request, I reported to the Captain's cabin. It was a sprawling room dominated by Captain Whyte's writing desk, his bunk and the officers' mess table. The latter was presently awash with several charts that would guide us to India in concert with the stars and the ship's sexton. With the great stern window to my right, I saluted as I stepped before the desk. After dismissing Bart, Captain Whyte grinned at me with a fatherly twinkle in his eye as he returned his quill pen to its stand.

"I do like you, lad."

"I'm honored, sir. The feeling is mutual," I added, still standing at attention.

"Is it?" he wondered. "Stand at ease and give me your answer."

As I assumed the more lax position, I guessed the Captain was testing me, as well as questioning my sincerity. He had no way of knowing that I was ever forthright. So this was his way of determining such a thing. Yet, I suspect he was also curious as to why I liked him.

"Aye, sir," I answered. "You're very much like my father—honest and fair to everyone you meet. That's the way I hope to be as well, and so you will be still another person for me to emulate, my father being the other."

"Well, that's admirable, Sam. Sam is right, isn't it?"

"Aye, sir."

"Well, Sam, I will tell you the same thing I told Webster and Dowell, the First and Second Mates. I do that because I want to know the feelings and stands of each of you before we sail. India is a long journey, and while, just now, I can't replace even one of you because of the Lord Governor's impatience for his staff, I will promise to do that, once we reach Calcutta, is that fair?"

"Most fair, sir," I said and nodded, wondering what I was about to hear. "Please tell me your views, Captain, you've made me curious to hear them."

"Ahh, so you have the patience to be curious, do you? Still more reason for me to think you *might* work out. Webster is impatient for his own command, while John Dowell is the sort who becomes impatient if tea is late." After we exchanged understanding smiles on the latter, he continued, "I suppose I can understand how Webster feels, but I am more concerned about Dowell since we have such a lengthy voyage ahead of us."

"I see what you mean, Captain. Dowell's impatience could readily explode in anger that would be bad for morale."

"Yes, it would," he agreed with an admiring smile. "Still, just because you understand that, doesn't necessarily mean that you adhere to such a philosophy. So must I be concerned for you in the same way?"

"Such concern would be wasted on me, sir."

"Oh? Why is that? You seem to speak from experience. You seem to appreciate the need for patience, even though this is your first voyage."

I shook my head and replied, "No, it isn't, sir. When I was twelve, Bart's age, I travelled to America and back with my father, and that journey planted the seed of my love for the sea."

"So you love the sea, eh?—*splendid!* Yes, I think you and I will get along very well. Still, I owe you an explanation of my views on the Navy, and then I wish to hear your feelings on them."

"Please, proceed, Captain Whyte."

"Thank you, lad," he said, before he lit his long white pipe, while urging me to pull up one of the nearby chairs and use it. When I was comfortable, he began, "To be frank and to the point, I absolutely detest what passes for discipline in this navy. Beatings for minor offenses are not the way to make a man an integral part of a crew. Indeed, they rob him of any hope of being efficient in his work because he will soon come to hate that labor, while he will ever fear his superiors and dislike them for the pain inflicted. If too many such men dislike their officers in such a way, then the ship's effectiveness as a military unit disappears. Do you see that?"

"I do, sir. To me, it would be far better to punish a man by having him do something practical, like polishing the ship's bell," I observed.

The Captain nodded at my suggestion and said, "Conversely, I believe that if you treat a person properly, they will respond in kind. Indeed, they will go out of their way to give you a good effort. Do you agree, Sam?"

"Definitely, sir."

"Good," he said with a smile. "I think you and I *do* understand each other. Yet, just so we *are* clear, I will confirm that on this ship there will be no such abuse of men or officers. In fact, it is my hope that you will treat all those on board *Breeze* with respect and humanity, regardless of their rank. Now, do I sense from what I saw on deck, and from what you have said just now, that you, Lieutenant Dawes, will have *no trouble* with that philosophy?"

"None, sir. My father taught all of us to behave like that towards others. He was especially interested that my oldest brother learn that since Matthew will take over the business some day, and since Father naturally hopes that his hat factory will prosper for all of the right reasons. Among those reasons, is what you just implied—that a well-treated person will always be more alert and quick-minded, which makes he or she more efficient, a better worker, a better crewman."

The Captain grinned and noted, "Well said! Now since Mr. Webster and Mr. Dowell don't agree with me, it is my hope that you will act as my liaison with the crew until the seamen learn to trust me. If you perform such duty well, I will see that you are First Mate when we leave Calcutta. What do you say to that?"

"That I will do all I can to earn the honor, sir. Might I start by going topside and relieving Mr. Webster?"

"Indeed, you might!" he replied with a beam.

⌘⌘⌘

Chapter IV

TO CALCUTTA

T TOOK WELL over a year for *Breeze* to journey from England to India and then to America. With Webster and Dowell on board for the leg to Calcutta, the first part of our journey might have been a most unpleasant time. Yet, that never happened because Captain Whyte and myself would not allow it to degrade into a series of cruelties toward anyone. At first, we had used words to assure the men that it would not be so. The Captain even encouraged the men to sing while they worked, as long as the songs were good-natured. Initially, none of the men took advantage of that liberty.

Then, early on in the voyage, as we began to pass Africa, Webster claimed that one of the sailors had improperly addressed him. It seemed that after the First Mate had taken a turn around the main deck, he started to go below. Seaman Watson had just scrubbed down that very flight of steps as part of his duty. As Lieutenant Webster started down those steps, Watson, without looking to see who was coming, urged, *Watch where you step!* Webster objected that the warning was far too harsh, and that it did not include the proper form of address, meaning *sir* or *Lieutenant*. Both men admitted that the incident had taken place as described, while Watson conceded that his warning might have been abrasive because he was a bit annoyed that someone would tramp through his good efforts, and that that same person ought to be more cautious, given the slippery nature of the stairs just then.

With the Captain, Lieutenant Dowell, and myself serving as the Board of Inquiry, it was then for us to discuss and arrive at a verdict. John Dowell was, of course, ready to condemn Watson to twenty lashes. I reminded the Captain that Lieutenant Webster had acted with a careless disregard. He could, as Watson had observed, very easily have slipped on one of the steps, which were still damp, and fallen on Watson, which would have injured both. I also asked the Captain to put himself in Watson's position, where the man had been laboring on those steps for some while, and then here comes Webster to ruin the work in an instant.

Nodding, Captain Whyte looked at the assembled crew, at the accused, and then, at the accuser, and pronounced, "Seaman Watson, we find you guilty of improper conduct—next time don't be so *harsh* with the tone of your warning. Then, after giving that warning, stand ready to help the intruder. Is that understood, man?"

"Aye, sir," the sailor said with a proper acknowledgment that he had contributed to the incident.

"Good," our master judged as he smiled. "I hereby sentence you to polishing the ship's bell."

The crew cheered the sentence, while Lieutenant Webster began to whine, until the Captain commanded, "Mr. Webster!—come to attention!"

That silenced everyone although the First Mate seemed to question the command, even though he obeyed it. He did not enjoy taking orders as much as he liked giving them. Yet, that time he was also a bit concerned about what was to befall him, and so it was, that he trembled a bit as he awaited the Captain's remarks. In a way, it reminded me of his reaction to his lapse about signing in Tibbs and me.

"Lieutenant Webster, you are *also* found guilty," the Captain said, which stunned most of those assembled there. "You are guilty of not thinking about the wisdom of descending a slippery stairway. Safety is a high priority on board this ship, and this act demonstrates a blatant disregard for safety on your part. I also agree that your carelessness ruined Watson's efforts, and that you are guilty of being inconsiderate toward him. Therefore, you will also be sentenced."

"What?" Webster raged.

"Calm yourself, Lieutenant, or I may take offense."

Webster briefly thought about fuming, but he realized that Captain Whyte could court martial him then and there for insubordination, especially since a Board of Inquiry was already convened, and since the Captain and I made up the majority on that Board. Steadily, the First Mate composed himself while the onlookers continued to mumble. Lieutenant Dowell, of course, had been just as livid, but he was too much of a coward to challenge the Captain.

"All right, sir, what is my sentence?" Webster asked.

"You are to shake the hand of Seaman Watson and apologize for your careless disregard of his person and his efforts."

"And if I refuse?" Webster cried.

"Then you will be deemed insubordinate, and I will have you confined to your cabin for the balance of the voyage to Calcutta," the Captain answered. "Now, carry out your punishment. That *is* an order! Remember, insubordination is an indelible stain."

Of course, at first, several of the men muttered that the sentence was too lenient. Then, when all of them began to realize how much Lieutenant Webster disliked his punishment, they began to smile and nod toward Captain Whyte with approval. Things *would* be different on board *Breeze*.

I suppose some sympathy could be found for the Lieutenant. The Captain had chosen the punishment in an effort to embarrass Webster into thinking about his regard for others. Yet, I think sympathy would be wasted if the First Mate failed to learn his lesson. With his face red and his head down, Webster blindly stuck his hand out to Watson and mumbled what sounded like an apology. Being far nobler, Watson also apologized as he briefly shook the offered hand and thanked the First Mate.

"That squares it, Captain," Watson agreed.

"Good, lad. Mr. Webster, in the future, I trust you will be more careful as you go about this ship. What is more, if a problem can be resolved with a little consideration and understanding, then it should be so addressed by the parties involved. If nothing else, call over Lieutenant Dawes or myself to mediate, before you get so worked up that you can think of nothing but filing charges on what are otherwise relatively trivial problems."

Of course, neither the First nor the Second Mate cared for any of that. They clearly hated the liberal way in which that cruise was conducted. It may be that the Navy agreed with them, and had us assigned to America for the main part of our duty because of Captain Whyte's views. Yet, that incident had also taught Webster and Dowell that Captain Whyte was not to be trifled with, and that I would always be in league with our master. They could also readily guess that the crew sided with us, which let out the recourse of mutiny. That crewmen, in steadily increasing numbers, began to sing as they worked was further evidence of where their allegiance lay. It was also shortly after that incident that, with the Captain's permission, I joined Tibbs in climbing up to the crow's nest on the foremast early one morning.

"You first, Tibbs, and you're to take your normal spot," I directed.

"Aye, sir," he responded although still a bit uneasy.

We then steadily ascended both ratlines, drawing curious looks as we went. At the same time, those looks, nearly all from seamen, were tinged with appreciation for what I was doing. Typically, the rigging is the domain of the men, while the officers are meant to hold to the deck. Yet, these men also knew my thinking was as liberal as the Captain's, which was reason enough for none of them to frown in condemnation for my actions that morning. They were in keeping, and it seemed reasonable to the men to suspend judgment until I had accomplished all of my designs for that climb.

Tibbs, as you might guess, was quick to arrive at the same conclusion, and after he had taken his seat on the board where it fronted the mast, he advised, "Take hold of the railing first, sir, and then sit with your legs dangling over the edge. Be sure to keep at least one hand on the railing at all times. That and sitting are for your safety, something Captain Whyte ordered me to do, just before I began my first duty up here, and before he told me what he expected me to do."

As I settled in, after carefully heeding Tibbs's cautions, I noted, "Yes, I can see where this is the safest posture." Then I looked out over the broad expanse, still tinged with the pink of dawn on our left, to port, and I added, "I can also see where this a wondrous place."

"Aye, sir, it's also the best place to come if you want to put things into proper perspective, it is."

"Well said, Tibbs!" I noted.

As I looked through the compass, still marveling at the glorious panorama, my chest swelled with an even greater awe than I had known when eyeing the bustle of Portsmouth. The latter was a cornucopia of human making, while what lay before me on my first visit to Tibbs's station was a far-reaching product of the Maker. The difference was readily apparent to me, and just as consuming. It was truly a wonder to behold.

"So, Tibbs, how do you keep yourself from being so over-whelmed by all this, so that you can maintain your vigilance for other ships and the like?"

He looked at me, not with confusion, but with an appreciative wonder that grew from being asked to share his craft with another. He readily liked the idea of being able to teach another how to per-form his daily task. He also relished the fact that I seemed so will-ing to learn from him. Yet, in the next instant, when he accepted the proposition of teaching me, our relationship was forever changed. We were no longer officer and man. I think it was that moment when we became friends.

"Well, sir," he began, knowing that that change did not end his need for a proper regard, "as you know the term *look through the compass* means that your eyes go from extreme left to extreme right and back. I take it a step further, I do. I start by looking at the extreme left just above the horizon, and then keeping that level, I slowly scan to the extreme right. But, rather than go back across at that level, I drop down to the line of the horizon, and use that level. Then, when I reach the extreme left, I drop still further down, be-fore I scan back to the extreme right. Finally, I reverse the entire process until I get back to extreme left above the horizon. I do it that way because it doesn't allow me to lapse into daydreaming, which neither of us wants, right?"

"True enough. I will pass that onto the Captain."

"No need, sir, since the Captain was the one to tell me about that, knowing I would be newborn to the crow's nest. Thanks, nonetheless."

"Of course, Tibbs. At the same time, I do observe that while your routine may be the Captain's idea, it is most clear to me by now that you do a splendid job of implementing it."

"Thank you, sir. I've heard and seen good things about you as well, which leads me to think you'll be an excellent First Mate."

Indeed, on reaching India, Webster and Dowell quickly found other ships, while, as the Captain had promised, I was promoted to First Mate, and we found a pair of more tolerable officers to make the journey to America.

***

THOSE TWO OFFICERS were Jenkins and Newton, who signed on as Second and Third Mates. That voyage to the New World showed both of them the value and correctness of our philosophy. That and the nature of our assignment in America also encouraged both to commit to extended service.

So, on reaching America, a wonderful succession of years followed as we plied between Boston, New York, Philadelphia, Charleston and Yorktown, which served the Virginian capital of Williamsburg. We also touched the wharves of the growing communities of Providence and Baltimore. Letters, packages and small loads of goods were the principals of our journeys, but on a more and more frequent basis, we also carried passengers. Men named Washington, Adams, Jefferson and Paine, who openly applauded Captain Whyte's views on discipline, and then boldly revealed their thoughts on the growing friction between the Colonies and Parliament. It was a topic on the minds of many because not a few Colonists were beginning to lose their patience with the tax policies of the Crown.

George Washington was the most interesting of all our passengers. Not only was he a figure of extraordinary stature, at a time when men averaged five-and-a-half feet in height, but also that six-foot-two gentleman possessed marvelous strength and fairly glowed with success. Further, there was something about him—a charisma, if you will—that commanded one's absolute respect and attention.

My first sense when I met him was that he was destined to be a man of greatness. That meeting occurred not long after we had departed Yorktown for Philadelphia. He and Captain Whyte were seated at the officers' mess table in the great cabin while they enjoyed coffee, molasses cookies and a bowl of walnuts. To this day, I don't know if that meeting occurred because I wanted it to, or because I was drawn to the cabin by Washington's presence. What I needed to tell the Captain was of little consequence. He knew me to be capable, and he knew that I could manage the ship in any situation. So, there was really no reason, short of an emergency, to go down to his cabin that morning.

"Our course is set, sir, and Tibbs has been posted to the foremast," I reported.

"Very good, Lieutenant. Stand at ease and meet Colonel George Washington, a member of the House of Burgesses."

The tall Virginian grinned and stood up to shake my hand. At his height, he towered a good three inches above me as he extended his arm. His hand grasped mine with a firm resolve that I shall never forget. Nor will I forget my confusion over that first meeting when I felt a strong compulsion to straighten up and salute, even though he was clad in a blue suit.

"Honored, Colonel," I added, with a slight bow of my head, correctly sensing that he would find a bow less embarrassing than a salute.

"As am I, Sam. Does that surprise you?"

"It does, sir," I answered.

"Well, it shouldn't, since a gentleman should always be honored to meet another gentleman. That is the way of our breed, and I trust you will remember that."

"Indeed, I will, sir."

"Good," Colonel Washington said with a grin. "Now have you left the main deck in good hands?"

"I have."

"Then why not join Captain Whyte and me for some refreshments? We were exchanging views on Parliament's treatment of the Colonies."

Uncertain of how to reply, I glanced at the ship's master, and when the Captain nodded, I accepted the invitation and was quickly asked to share my thoughts on the topic, to which I responded, "Well, I've always felt that Parliament should've listened to Benjamin Franklin and let the Colonies defend themselves during the last war with the French. As it was, the Colonies did take part in that defense, and that should be taken into consideration. Instead, even though the war was also fought in other parts of the world, Parliament wants the Colonies to bear the *full* cost, and Parliament has been overly unreasonable by continuing this parade of attempts to make the Colonies do just that, no matter how severely they protest, as with the tea dumping incident in Boston."

Both men grinned, and George Washington asked, "Do you see these protests ending in the Colonies breaking with England?"

"Well, I can't blame them, especially if Parliament keeps backing the Colonies into a corner. What else can they do?"

Again, both men smiled, and so we continued to share our views. Those views made the rounds of the crew, and it was not hard for me to see that all of us found sympathy with the Colonies in the dispute. At the same time, thanks to the several radicals we ferried from port to port, that sympathy for the plight of the Colonists steadily changed to alliance. Then, not long after the Rebels laid siege to Boston in April 1775, I again stepped before the Captain's desk and saluted.

He looked up from noting in his logbook that we were nearing Philadelphia, and with an expectant grin, asked, "What is the word, Sam?"

"Sir, after talking to all of the men and officers, it is my opinion that most, if not all, mean to seize the ship and offer it to the Rebels with themselves as crew. I include myself in that number."

"As do I. Yet, we must proceed with some caution. America breaking with England is so far not the intent of this fight. If this ship and crew turn Rebel, and there is no break, we would all hang for desertion. No, I say that, unless we are ordered to stop serving as a mail packet, that we should continue in our present role, and see what comes of waiting. However, I do think we should test the waters by talking to our radical friends at Philadelphia to see what they think we should do."

I agreed and saw that the rest of the crew understood the need for tact. Our Rebel friends in Philadelphia and elsewhere agreed with our prudent course and promised to keep us apprised of developments. In the meantime, we continued our role as packet, until America declared her independence, which coincided with our unanimous declaration to side with the Rebels.

From then on, we sailed and fought in the name of America, with a pride that easily surpassed our pride in ourselves and our ship, and to go with our new role, we gave the ship a new name...*Scorpion!*

✳✳✳

WE WERE TIED up in Philadelphia when we officially joined the Rebels to fight what had become a war for independence. Due to our proximity and the known politics of our crew, Congress had a ready response for us. As *Scorpion*, we were to serve the United States as a privateer with Boston as our homeport. With those initial orders, came a working definition of privateer that spelled out how Congress expected us to do our job. There was also a caution against taking on too big a foe. Of course, the assignment was really not that much of a surprise, since we had discussed such a role on more than one occasion with our radical friends. So we returned to the sea, and before long, we had taken our first prize.

Few of us will forget that initial success. Ironically, it came just a year before our encounter with *Graywolf*. We were again plying the waters off Boston, not far from the shipping lanes that led down to Long Island and New York. Tibbs, as ever, was at his post as we rode through another sparkling Summer day.

"Three sails, Captain!" he called from his nest.

Captain Whyte learned the direction and called for general quarters, while I took the helm. Steadily, we came up on the pair of merchantmen being escorted by the British bark *Richmond*, which looked to be a true sister ship of *Scorpion*. Knowing we were evenly matched, our master chose to come up on the threesome without displaying our colors, but with both batteries of guns ready to fire. Surprise would give us the advantage.

Richmond was leading her larger charges on a generally southwest course. By design, we came up on them from the north, or at a forty-five degree angle. Naturally, they were suspicious of us. We were a lone warship, coming out of nowhere, and so, as we drew within range, they signaled for us to display our colors or risk a fight.

We answered by hoisting our flag with the starry blue corner and red and white stripes, and with a broadside from our port guns. That blast shredded the main sail of *Richmond*'s foremast, ruined a gun and left huge gouges in her starboard side. Then, just as that first spray of a dozen rounds arched through the air, Captain Whyte had me pivot us to the northeast, which let our starboard guns fire on *Richmond*. That firing knocked out two more of her starboard guns and damaged her helm. By the time we had swung around to give them another broadside from our port guns, *Richmond*'s Captain had realized that he couldn't maneuver, which meant we could pick apart his weakened right side until he sank or surrendered. So he ordered their colors struck.

Not long after that, a long boat from *Richmond* had pulled her on course before we escorted all three ships to Boston. By shadowing our captives off their starboard sides, and even with the third, we were positioned to keep any of them from entertaining thoughts of flight. Further, having lost their escort, the Captains of the merchantmen realized they could fall prey to other ships hunting on those waters—ships that might not be as merciful.

So, in good order, we brought them to Boston where our success was soundly cheered. There, *Richmond* was repaired, given a new crew, and renamed *Viper,* as it joined our fleet of privateers. The other ships and their cargoes were taken to the auction block. Of course, by the time the fate of all three had been resolved, *Scorpion* was again patrolling the shipping lanes. Our good fortune had been applauded and appreciated, and that was enough for us.

After a few more months of such activity, which was noted by more successes, and with Winter drawing nigh, Captain Whyte relinquished his command to me, so he could better help the infant American Navy establish itself by serving as an advisor to Congress. By the time we encountered *Graywolf, Scorpion* had taken eight more prizes, defeating three British brigs and one more bark in the process. Our success soon made us more than just an annoyance to the British, especially since the captive sailors were regularly swapped as the two sides exchanged prisoners. Those seamen were compelled to reveal who had captured them, and so, after enough mentions, *Scorpion* became a scourge to the British. That meant that, in time, the King would almost certainly dispatch one or two frigates to hunt *Scorpion* into extinction. If so, it meant tying up those ships when they might be used elsewhere, and that would let us serve America in a different way.

On the other hand, I wondered if the successful return of Lord Cornwallis's niece would somehow alter British designs on us. That seemed most unlikely. Yet, whatever happened, we would follow our present orders until we received new ones, or until we rode our ship to its watery grave. It mattered not what our fate was to be. We were in it *together*, and that was always a comfort.

Further, we all sincerely believed that we were honoring God and country, in the best way we could, with our heroic stance in that time of war and the fabled quest for liberty.

⌘ ⌘ ⌘

Chapter V

WITHOUT FAIL

UNDAUNTED BY CIRCUMSTANCE, or possible outcome—both highly unmanageable factors—we kept alive our quest of chasing down *Graywolf*. On through the starspeckled ebony of night, beyond the brilliant red robes of Aurora, and into the first hours of daylight, which were ornamented with low clouds, we sailed without thought of quitting. No, we steadily pursued the pirate through the clock of that day and on through a second night, even when, late on the second morning of our pursuit, the deck began to heave and roll in a more pronounced manner. Still, we entertained no notion of ending the hunt.

As for the steadily rising swell, none of us really minded sailing into bad weather. We were, first of all, sailors. We had all been through rough weather before, and we would be again. It was part of our profession.

In some ways, a storm at sea provides a wonderful challenge. Not only must the helmsman try to maintain our course, but he also must be alert to strong contrary winds that could easily snap one of the straining masts, and he must endeavor to sail *over* the waves, not between them. Yet, nothing can keep seawater from spilling on the deck. As a result, the main deck, which can rise and fall at incredible angles, becomes so slippery that a simple walk from a hatch to one of the side rails is transformed into an arduous trek. A network of newly secured ropes made such a trek less trying, while helping each of us to continue carrying out our tasks on the deck. Aloft, Tibbs and the others clung tighter to lines, railings or yardarms without thought of coming down until the order was given to do so. Discipline became a valued ally under those circumstances.

At the same time, while it was hardly necessary for me to warn my crew to be careful or to instruct them on what to do, I nevertheless did since that was always the way of sea Captains. We had to lead and remind, no matter how experienced the crew. Indeed, the men expected me to do as much, just as they expected me to urge them to maintain the cleanliness of the ship. That was my part. Joining them in the bow to listen to them sing, simply reaffirmed that, as the ship's master, I likened myself to Captain Whyte. Yet, also like him, my reminders were neither harsh nor derisive.

After another hour of rough sea that second morning, the sky had darkened and lowered. A strong surge of wind filled our sails, while waves, foaming mad, began to crash over the bow. They flung their spray the length of the deck, and after a great heave and fall of the deck, they passed on, one at a time, like solemn marchers. Also about then, sheets of rain began to fall, driven hard by the wind. With a relentless disregard, they soaked all of us and further degraded the visibility. Still, we kept sailing onward, following *Graywolf*. In the meantime, the sea had become a murky green marked by curling mountains of water that raged toward us with princely white crowns. More and more, the blackness overhead stood out in a contrast that was as sharp as the sudden flash of lightning and the great boom of thunder.

It was not unlike a battle in that way, but at the same time, I knew from experience that storms could be far more terrible. They could not be intimidated by a uniform blast of guns. They did not give up. They merely moved on, while you were left to your own devices, no matter how badly your ship was ruined. If, after being in a good gale, you somehow made it to the nearest port, then you could lay up until repairs had made you seaworthy. Otherwise, if you failed to make it to port, the sea would become your ship's grave and, most likely, yours as well.

That was all the incentive necessary to put every effort into getting your ship through a storm, no matter how wet or tired you became. Keeping the ship in top shape by routinely cleaning and maintaining all of it, in much the way you would maintain your home, meant the ship was always ready to endure the rigors of a storm, much less those of war. How long could we endure if we lost a spar in the first good gust from a storm because we had been lax, or if we lost a sheet because it wasn't properly furled?

So, without question or hesitation, men went aloft, while others stood by on the deck ready to go where directed by one of the Mates or myself. All of us clung to lines more firmly, but never said a thing about the need to continue our tasks. Pride in the ship, engendered from maintaining her, and pride in what we were doing, whether our current quest or the greater one to preserve our nation, were paramount to everyone. So it was, that even those stationed below, to watch for leaks that might become worse and to pump water out at need, never shirked when it became their turn to go aloft in foul weather.

Now, despite the deteriorating weather, *Graywolf* was more visible to us. The storm's merciless strain on her cracked mainmast had forced the rogues to furl canvas, thereby slowing her progress. By one that afternoon, she was no more than a thousand yards ahead. I was glad of that since, by then, the weather had forced me to order Tibbs down from his aerie, along with all of the other hands aloft. Experience told me that we had made ourselves fit to ride it out as best we could, while our quarry was readily visible.

There *is,* of course, a point when you have to trust in God being merciful. He knows whether or not you have done your best to help yourself out of a difficult situation, and so He knows when mercy has been earned. Certainly, that was true on that fateful day in our history, and it was further true that God would likely appreciate our attempt to right a wrong by saving Miss Walton. Aye, we were, one and all, Samaritans turned aside to lend a hand, never mind the politics or origin of the woman we sought to help.

Still, I felt that even if we lost sight of the pirate, we knew her course and could guess her destination well enough to maintain the chase. Unfortunately, the latter would likely spell a sad fate for Miss Walton. No, we had to make every effort to keep *Graywolf* in view. That, after the safety of my ship and crew, was my first concern. At the same time, I knew my crew would expect a fair degree of hazard, which was reason enough to maintain the chase regardless of the weather. They also knew, to the man, that I would never expose them to excessive hazard without reason—calling them down when the ship was secured against our present storm reminded all of them of that philosophy.

The only other care I had then was that the pirate's captain, in his madness, was leading all of us into an impossible situation, while challenging us to defeat him by adopting his madness. By that, I mean that just ahead of the brig, I could now see the blackest of skies I had ever witnessed. Frequent fans of sheet lightning showered the ebony horizon with sharp glimmers as both ships violently heaved over and through the foaming pyramids of green. Yet, I knew our strength and character, and so, I quietly urged our helm, Mr. Newton, to steadily maintain our course.

Still, the brig would not turn. The fiend held to her course as if daring us to follow. My only hope was that our stormy encounter would be brief. Then *Graywolf* entered the black weather, and to my amazement, the pirate seemed to be completely consumed by it. It was as if she had gone through a heavy curtain of black cloth, and in a manner of speaking, she had.

Some five minutes later, the black cloud engulfed *Scorpion*, as well. At first, all we could see was the cloud, which seemed to enshroud our ship, and the sea, which was dominated by giant waves that smashed across our bow. Still stranger was the way the waves marched toward us as if on parade, and the way that they themselves had become black. Light, itself, seemed to be absent. Perhaps, even God could not penetrate that ebony cloak. It appeared that we had reached the extreme of hazard.

Indeed, it seemed to me that we had entered a tunnel through sky and water. Adding to the prevailing eeriness, walls of lightning, accompanied by shivering rolls of deafening thunder, fell on either side of the ship, but oddly never even threatened either the tips of our yardarms or the tops of the masts. There has never been a more bizarre moment in my life or that of *Scorpion*. Yet, knowing now what happened to us, I cannot help but feel that that was as it should be.

"Steady, men!—we'll manage!" I called out as I clung to my line near the port rail, while the men hovered near the feet of the six main ratlines, ready to spring aloft if dire circumstance commanded me to so order them. "Steady on, Mr. Newton!—steady on!"

"Aye, sir!" cried the Mate in reply.

The bad weather alone had not dictated my assignment of the Mates to the wheel, round the clock. No, our closing with *Graywolf* had brought on that decision. It seemed only logical and more efficient to have one of them at the wheel, while we were nearing the moment of an active encounter with the pirate. That way, the same person could continue to man the helm if we went into battle.

"Sir, look!" he cried and pointed ahead.

I was indeed surprised at what I saw—the great black cloud was giving way to gray sky, and not far beyond the gray, we could see a circle of sunshine and blue skies, with *Graywolf* perfectly silhouetted against them.

∗∗∗

IN LESS THAN five minutes, we had found the sunshine as well, which naturally cheered all of us. For a while, the darkness had been the pirates' ally, hiding it and its troublesome designs from God and His servants. Now the storm and gloom were gone, replaced by the glorious light of the daystar, and *that* was our ally. As well as raising our spirits, that steadfast, caring glow also allowed us to better see our foe.

I was further glad to see that *Graywolf*'s lead had shrunk to seven hundred yards. Using my glass from near our starboard bow, I began to understand why. Despite her crew's attempt to ease the strain during the storm, her mainmast was swaying fitfully, the crack, caused by our hit, having grown, thanks to the brief, but violent, storm, while the mast's shrouds had lost their tautness.

Was that a sign meant to show us that we were indeed favored by God in this incident? If so, I welcomed His help and vowed to make us worthy of it by successfully completing our current mission. Then we would further honor God by encouraging the other American privateers, through Congress if necessary, to always be ready to help defeat the dark designs of a pirate.

"Land, ho!—dead ahead, sir!" Tibbs cried, not long after carefully retaking his still slippery post atop the foremast.

"I see it, Tibbs!" I returned.

Graywolf was making for the island, which was one of the Bahamas. I was certain that if we caught the rogues before they slipped into the nearest port, we could ruin their plans for Miss Walton. That certainly would make things much simpler as far as we were concerned. It would also save their captive from some unspeakable torment. No, we wanted to retake her without any harm coming to her. That was the best we could hope for, and since we were all good-hearted, it was also how we wanted things to end. So, with the gap between the ships steadily shrinking, I knew our opportunity to achieve the preferred outcome was at hand.

With Mr. Newton still at the helm, I commanded, "General quarters, Mr. Jenkins!"

"Aye, sir!" the dark-haired First Mate answered and went to ring the bell as I began striding back toward the helm.

"Aim a bit to the left, lads," I told the starboard gunners as I passed them. "Aim a bit to the right, friends," I told those on the port side.

By the time the gunners announced their readiness, *Graywolf* was just a mile from the island, while we had closed to within five hundred yards of the pirate. That was within range, but by the time we swung to fire a broadside, we'd be out of range—we had to keep closing. My guess was that we would get one chance, and that our best hope was to somehow finish off their mainmast. With that spar downed, they'd lose their mizzen, which would hurt their maneuverability, and of course, they would lose a great deal of their speed. Then, with *Graywolf* slowed and difficult to turn, we could easily close, fire another broadside or two, and maneuver to board her. It was a straightforward plan, but shoals, in the form of intangibles, could play a role.

By the time the guns were ready, I had instructed Mr. Jenkins to stand in the bow where he was to fix his eyes on *Graywolf*'s rudder and wave the appropriate arm, indicating the direction of her turn, the moment she began to pivot in preparation for shadowing the coast of the island. Then, on my reaching the helm, Mr. Newton learned his assignment that included how he was to respond to the First Mate's wave. Since I had absolute faith in both of them, I saw no need to take on either task myself. Instead, I stood near the helm, where I could watch my plan unfold and be ready to take the wheel should anything unfortunate happen to the

Second Mate. Our quick response to general quarters that day, as on all days, was indeed a pleasure to me. I knew it had much to do with our long success as a privateer.

"Sir, look!" Mr. Jenkins cried and pointed ahead of *Graywolf.*

Several dozen odd-looking, swift-moving boats were streaking toward the pirate from the island, while it was not hard to notice a cluster of strangely dressed, half-naked people gathered on the beach that was straight ahead of us. Many of them were pointing our way, others at the pirate. The brig's starboard pivot gun boomed, casting a small ball that spewed a fountain of water not far from the little boats. With amazing agility, those same boats quickly turned and sped out of harm's way. Just as suddenly, Jenkins left arm shot out and began waving.

"To port, Mr. Newton!" I cried.

It was almost like we were dancing, the way our ships turned in unison. Now, though, instead of sailing single-file, we were sailing parallel, with *Graywolf* slightly ahead and well within range. The time had, indeed, come. Our one good chance was there for the taking. That moment, the one we had sought since first following after *Graywolf*, was before us.

"Starboard gunners!—fire!" I shouted.

Our guns roared in disciplined unison. Smoke, white and sulfuric, billowed up over our rigging and canvas. The sight and sound of that broadside turned many heads, to include those of the people on the beach and in the quick boats. Arms from those same people were pointed our way, but not in a frenzied response like the pirates. Rather, they were gestures of wonder and curiosity. Those reactions and the small boats were the first clues that something had happened to us, but just then, none of us had the time to analyze what those hints meant. A sea battle did not permit one to think of anything else. It was a very jealous mistress, ever driven by Death, in the guise of a mad coachman.

In the meantime, one of our shot struck *Graywolf's* mainmast full on. With a loud crack, like the latest victim of a lumberjack's axe, that spar fell toward us. The brig seemed to shutter in pain as that tree of human making slammed down on the raised quarter-deck, the spar jutting out over the port stern. In the meantime, our other twelve-pound spheres of iron slammed into the raised quarterdeck spewing splinters and smoke into the air; into gun carriages, which upset the brass cannon barrels mounted on top of them; and into gruff, snarling men, killing or maiming them.

Six of the brig's nine portside cannon answered in poor unison, and all of their rounds either whistled overhead or fell harmlessly into the sea. *Graywolf* was outmatched in every way imaginable: guns, discipline, ability, speed, maneuverability, determination, and, of course, teamwork. They could not hope to best us, but then, they were not the kind who surrendered.

No, their only reward for surrendering was a noose thrown over the nearest yardarm. Knowing that, I realized they could become as dangerous as cornered rats, but I also sensed that they could only intimidate the weak and helpless, which meant they would respond with desperation and great concern to someone like us. Their desperation could make them err, to our advantage. What's more, a ship of disciplined, courageous sailors, armed with cannon, muskets, pistols, and sabers would more likely be something *they* feared! That may have been reason enough for them to sail us into bad weather, hoping we would either not follow, or that we would be dashed to pieces by the storm.

Yet, while so much as one ruffian and one gun remained to her, *Graywolf* could bully the world and be even more of a nuisance than we ever could. We did not loot our prizes, nor did we harm their passengers. When we brought them to Boston, the latter were usually released with apologies provided—not sold to the highest bidder. The distinction between what we did and what the pirate did was clear, and I hoped that Miss Walton would understand enough of that, so she could make an accurate report to her uncle.

That report would not necessarily save us from being hunted down by the British. I doubted that even her safe return would prevent that. We were too successful. But if she could at least convince them that we ourselves weren't pirates, then that might save all of us from the noose. Further, I did hope that her observations would help to legitimize our efforts and those of our young nation.

"To starboard, Mr. Newton! Port guns!—stand ready! Muskets!—stand ready!"

The turn brought us angling across our foe's stern, while the pirate could now only hold to her present course. Our cannoneers stood ready with their matches, while up above, Tibbs and his men began to raise their muskets in anticipation of my command. The time for a new round of action was almost at hand. We had to be ready to respond to it, in much the way we had responded to our sail through the storm, a short time before.

Like the storm, we had done much to slow and cripple the pirate. After another good pounding, it would likely be time to finish her off. That was still more reason for all hands on *Scorpion* to be alert and ready to respond. Circumstances, even more than my commands, would demand such readiness and ability. I also expected willingness to be added into that mix when the time came.

Then, just as our foremast began to pass her starboard stern, I commanded, "Port guns!—fire!"

All twelve boomed in excellent precision. A new cloud of white, briefly obscuring the sunlight, rose up over our ship. With their skewed aim the port guns wound up strafing the length of our foe. One ball shattered the great window in the stern, another killed her helmsman, and a third smashed one of her long boats. The rest fell on still more of her guns and otherwise contributed to the battering she was sustaining. Further, I could see that her crew had been notably reduced, just as I could see that their ship was quickly becoming a derelict. We had to resolve our fight, before she became a hazard.

The time had come to utterly end *Graywolf*'s infamous moment in *Scorpion*'s life, and in the annals of human writing.

✳✳✳

WITH THAT, THOUGH, the time had come for the most difficult and dangerous of all naval military operations. I mean, of course, boarding an enemy ship with designs of seizing control of her, and forcing her crew to surrender. As mentioned, we knew that none of the pirates would ever surrender, which meant a fight to the death from all of them. Just as well, we really had no accommodations for a horde of prisoners.

On the other hand, in all the time that we had served as a privateer, we had never boarded another ship because Congress would not permit it unless the other ship was in danger of sinking, or unless some similar circumstance prevailed, as it did with *Graywolf*. That was meant to keep us from entertaining thoughts of gain through looting, rape, and kidnap. Cruel murders also promoted the barbaric image of our current foes, while furthering the terror that all innocent sea travellers felt on seeing that black flag unfurled. Yet, our inexperience in boarding would never preclude our attempting such a feat in the case of *Graywolf*. It was the only way to finish her off, recover Miss Walton, and return to Boston.

"To port, Mr. Newton! Bring us alongside," I said to the Second Mate, before I called to the rest of the crew, " Muskets!—find your targets and fire! Everyone else!—prepare for boarding!"

As we turned back and drew toward their starboard side, four of their guns on that side fired. One blew up and killed its crew, a second sent a ball glancing off our far rail, while the other two lobed their projectiles across our deck and into the water. In the meantime, the two-dozen surviving rogues began to prepare a defense of their ship, although our musketeers, led by Tibbs, as they fired from aloft, thwarted the pirates' defensive preparations. Indeed, my friend's sharp eyes and steady nerves made him the best shot of the crew.

That fire from above forced the pirates to cower in two parties, one near the doors in front of their quarterdeck, and the other before the bow of *Graywolf*. That served to keep them away from the middle and facilitated the initial efforts of our boarding party. Three of my deck hands tossed grappling hooks to bind our ships side-to-side, while others laid down several wide planks that spanned the gap between the rails. Then, with pistols and swords drawn or pikes at the ready, most of us surged across the planks, while others swung over on loose lines. With our muskets still holding our foes at bay, the pirates could mount no concerted effort to block our final attempt on their ship.

"Be alert, men!—this could be rough!" I cautioned as I leapt down on *Graywolf*'s deck.

While Lieutenant Jenkins led a party toward the rogues cowering in the bow, I directed the rest in rushing the villains blocking the doors to the stern cabin under the quarterdeck. Our pistols downed a half dozen, before we met the remaining nine with our blades and pronged lances. None of our foes treated for mercy. They knew there was none for men of their repute. That should have made them bolder fighters, but not when they were really just blustering cowards armed with swords and knives—grown up bullies, if you will. We also outnumbered them by at least three to one, and so, we took advantage of them by ganging up on them.

As the last of the devils died defending the doors to the great cabin, those doors suddenly burst open, and there stood gristly Captain Barber with Miss Walton locked in his grasp and the tip of his rapier at her throat. He was the height of crudeness and vulgarity with a great, jeweled pin on either breast of his coat and drool glistening from his unmanaged beard. His beady, dark eyes might have made the weak quiver, but they had little effect on us, for not a man among us lowered his weapon or turned away out of fear. That lack of concern made his eyes widen as they darted about seeking an opening.

In the meantime, his dark-haired captive trembled for her life. Yet, she did smile at seeing all of us so ready to save her. That encouraged me to have hope, as did the fact that Captain Barber's glazed eyes suggested he was presently drunk. That was his weakness at present, and I saw a need to exploit it.

"Stand back!—I'll slice 'er if you don'. And that'd go ill with Lor' Cornwallis, it would!" he warned, trying to employ threats to get us to back down.

"Would it?" I returned as I held my ground and set a good example that my men readily emulated.

He looked my way and noted my ready cutlass, my epaulets, and my pistol. He also seemed to recognize from my uniform and manner that I was his counterpart. With that, most of his attention swung toward me. I was the one he had to deal with if he hoped to get away with something that day.

"In case you don't know, we're already at odds with Lord Cornwallis," I noted. "That's an American flag on our mizzen!"

"Pah!" he cried and spat. "Colorful rags are all the same to me! Only good for cleaning up *that!* Nay, I'm not fooled! You'd retch if I stuck her, whether you're at war with the Brits, or no."

Even though her pink dress was soiled, the dark-haired Miss Walton seemed entirely out of place as she shivered with fear. The edge of the pirate's blade was just inches from her long bare neck, threatening to gash it open, to further ruin her dress while taking her life. The terror in her eyes showed she was convinced the villain would do just that. My words of defiance had failed to rouse her courage. The grimy paw holding her like a great clamp was as much a deterrent, as was the gleaming point that could quickly end her life.

"Yes, Captain, you're right, " I admitted. "We would all be outraged if you slew Miss Walton. Certainly, your own life would be forfeit, but I suppose you expected that."

The sudden flash of concern in his eyes suggested that he had not. His life—however miserable—meant something to him. I wondered then if I could use that to bait him.

So I continued, "Still, we really have no further need to quarrel with you. We've slain your crew and ruined your ship. That doesn't mean we have to slay you, as well."

"What's that?" he cried with a revealing interest.

He was interested in only one thing. He dearly wanted to keep his life. Only that way could he get back to pillaging the seas.

"Well, it's simple. We'll trade you a boat for Miss Walton," I offered and paused to look back over my shoulder to see how the rest of my crew had faired.

The blackhearts atop *Graywolf*'s forecastle had all been slain. The ship was ours, save for the man before us. With luck, we would end his terrible rule on the seas, as well. It all depended on how well I could exploit his observed weaknesses.

Then I ordered, "Lads, four of you find a good boat and toss it over the starboard side, away from *Scorpion*. That's all right, do as I say." When four of them started toward the collection of boats lying near the center of the main deck, I turned back to Barber and said, "In the meantime, Captain, I'll trade places with Miss Walton."

With that, I put away my sword and tucked my pistol into my belt. Captain Barber's eyes narrowed. They had the beady quality of a rat's, while his scraggly, grimy person further added to that impression. He was as loathsome and contemptuous as a man could get. He was a pest who could easily frighten the weak of heart. Yet, it was uncertain how he would fight now that we had him backed into a corner. He could begin by slaying his hostage, especially if he thought he was going to die. On the other hand, I had offered him a chance to get out alive, and just then, that was all he really wanted. Would he take the offered bait, so he could scurry away to hide and wait until he found a new ship to infest, or would he reject it, dooming both Miss Walton and himself?

I stepped toward them, my left hand out. It grasped Miss Walton's wrist and started easing her out of her precarious situation. Barber's sword fell away. Her eyes swung up toward my face, but I kept mine on the Captain as, by design, I stepped between Miss Walton and him. His blade rose toward my neck. Suddenly, a splash erupted along the starboard side of *Graywolf* as my men dropped a boat overboard. Barber's eyes glanced toward the noise. The bait had been swallowed. As the rogue looked away, I stepped back, drew my pistol and fired, *blam!*

"God's blood!" he spat as he clutched his chest. With a grimace of pain, he looked at me and frothed, "I *knew* I couldn't trust you!"

"No more than I could trust you!" I returned as he fell back and lay dead in the open doorway to his cabin.

"Hurrah!" my crew cheered.

Yet, when loud, raucous applause and voiced jubilation erupted, we all looked toward the little boats and the beach. Our many onlookers seemed to be reacting as if they had witnessed the end of a play. Yet, there was a general rowdiness to the ovation that exceeded anything I had ever seen or heard in a theater. As that vocal display and the end of our fight allowed me to focus on those witnesses to our battle with *Graywolf*, I again noticed how scantily clad both the men and women were, and I noticed that many of their boats were made of a white material that was unfamiliar to me. Then I remembered my crew's need for direction, and our need to finish *Graywolf* before it became a peril to shipping.

"Is there anyone or anything else that needs to be rescued, Miss Walton?" I asked as I looked at her.

"No, I believe I was all they could manage to take from *Seacastle*, thanks to you and your ship, Captain," she said.

"I'm glad to hear that."

"Of course, these rascals didn't allow me much of a look at their ship before they locked me in a small cabin."

"Ohh, I see." Turning to my crew, I said, "Mr. Jenkins, take two men and set a charge in *Graywolf*'s magazine. As you return, take a look through the ship for anything of value. Also, call out to make sure no one else is on board."

"Aye, sir."

"The rest of you return to *Scorpion* and prepare to cast off. Miss Watson, allow me to help you across to our ship," I added and offered her my arm.

So, with a renewed bustle of activity, we got ready to part with the pirate that had led us into such unknown, mysterious waters.

⌘⌘⌘

Chapter VI

A FIND

CAREFULLY, I HELPED Miss Walton cross over to our ship. She appreciated my strong hand holding both of hers, while I pulled her along at an easy pace. Was it the sort of appreciation a young woman bestowed on a young man who interested her? It was difficult to say. While I had some experience in the ways of women, I had to ever remind myself that Miss Walton was part of a society that favored having, and keeping, divisions. Whatever regard she had for me was likely tempered by those mores, while we were further divided by politics and war, to say nothing of the fact that her uncle was a Lord. Then, when we reached the railing of *Scorpion*, I leapt down to the deck and easily lifted the young woman down from the plank. As I did, she blossomed into a smile, while her hands gently clung to my upper arms. It seemed her more immediate concerns had been put aside. Or was there more to her smile?

"What will you do now, Captain?" she asked as she stood at my side, free of any attachment to me.

"The First Mate, Lieutenant Jenkins, will inspect *Graywolf* and see to blowing it up, and then we'll return to Boston."

"Well, I am glad you told the First Mate to look through the ship. It now occurs to me that, as the rogues brought me through those doors to the main cabin, I did notice a great chest in Captain Barber's cabin. The box was open, and I could tell that something was reflecting light onto the lid from within. Certainly, you should have them look in that chest, and if it does hold loot, it is yours."

"I suppose we would have a claim to it. Hopefully, though, we will find a better use for it than our own gain," I said, before I looked toward the other ship. "Mr. Jenkins!"

"Aye, sir!" the First Mate called from the brig.

"Miss Walton recalls noting a great chest in the Captain's cabin. If it contains treasure, as she suspects, have Carson and Whitmore bring it across."

"Very good, Captain!" he replied and soon was directing his detail to go through the doors under the quarterdeck.

Moments later, their cries of jubilation preceded them as they returned through the doors. The two I had named were carrying a sizable box. I didn't have to see its contents to know what lay within. Their grins told me much. Yet, they were not smiles of avarice, but beams for a new facet of our success that day. Then the bearers carefully brought it across and took it down to my cabin.

I already had a good use in mind for that booty, and once we were on our way back to Boston, I meant to divulge that notion to the assembled crew. It was my sense that they would agree with my plan, especially since most of us believed that such money would only bring an ill wind and other troubles. Aye, it was tempting to suggest sharing it, but again, that was not our purpose, and I did not want my crew thinking of gain each time we sought to take a prize. That chest, as surely as *Graywolf*, would be an excellent test of our discipline as a military unit, as well as our unity as a crew. Could one of the deadly sins rise up to ruin that?

"No, Miss Walton, I think we will find a far better purpose for the contents of this box," I answered, knowing my crew.

"If that is the outcome, Captain, then I will gladly report to my uncle that, while *Scorpion* may be a great nuisance to our shipping, she is no pirate. That would allow all of you to keep your lives if you were ever defeated. In fact, I see where this ship is really just another part of your grand scheme to hold out until France intervenes. Uncle fears that that will happen."

Nodding, I conceded, "That is an accurate perception, all right. Well, come along, we should stand down by the helm until Mr. Jenkins's handiwork has dispatched *Graywolf*, unless you would prefer the comfort of my cabin."

"No, I shall be all right there by the helm, although I would feel more at ease if you would say something to these little boats about what you mean to do to the pirate."

"Why, thanks, for reminding me," I noted, glad to find her so concerned for others.

Too many Englishwomen of good family could easily distance themselves, intentionally or unintentionally, from the rest of society, the former being especially true if they were overly pampered. In a manner of speaking, they became isolated from reality, and from what it took to be truly human. Yet, in Miss Walton, I saw a caring woman who was independent enough to venture across the ocean on her own. Yet, I still doubted that she would find much interest in someone like me. I was at odds with her uncle, and whatever future I sought would either be with America, or for the time being, at the end of a British noose. Hers would likely be a proper marriage and a stately house to manage in London, and I would never suggest it should be otherwise.

Using my speaking trumpet, I then repeatedly told the boats to stand clear and alternated the warning between English and Spanish. As a further precaution, I had us maneuver so that we shielded the boats from the imminent blast. We had only just pulled in front of them when the brig's magazine went off. A ball of flame and a cloud of thick black smoke seemed to pull the deck and foremast several feet upward with them, while the ship's sides shattered. Then, split between its masts, the ship literally caved in down the middle, and finally, the two ends sank below the surface.

With that, *Graywolf* was gone. She took with her many corpses and even more villainy. If I had any regret, it was that the ship herself had never asked for such a role and fate. Only desperate and greedy men had corrupted the brig. Only courageous and righteous men could forever end *Graywolf*'s unwilling participation in such evil. Had our fight ended with her in better condition, I very seriously would have considered taking her back to Boston. There the brig almost certainly would be added to the small American fleet. There it would know a much better role—even a better fate—as it acted out its part in the great drama for independence and freedom.

I was about to give orders for us to set sail for Boston, when one of my men urgently called, "Captain!—over here!"

✳✳✳

I JOINED SEAMAN Garber at the starboard railing. As I did, he pointed to one of the small boats that had pulled to within twenty yards of that side. A man in beige shirt and pants—a uniform, I guessed—was standing on its bow with a red and white trumpet at his side. Like his three crewmen, the man was black, while his trumpet was made from an unfamiliar, shiny material, and there was a knob of like material inside its funnel that made me wonder how his trumpet could work with such a blockage. As for his boat, like the other small ones, it was constructed of a substance that looked like wood but was not wood. In addition, there was an odd lantern on its bow that flashed a red light on and off. When on, that light was steady and did not flicker, which suggested it was not some sort of candle or oil lamp. No, things were not as they should be. Those newest hints seemed to *add* to the mystery, rather than solve it.

When the Captain of the small boat noticed me, he put his trumpet to his lips, and asked, "Sir, what is your business with the Bahamas?"

Marveling at how well his trumpet projected his voice, I answered through mine, "Fate brought us to your waters, sir. Fate in the form of a pirate who had taken a woman hostage from a British merchantman bound for America. We gave chase, and that chase ended here."

Although he seemed rather perplexed by my explanation, he still managed to ask, "So then you fought the pirate, saved the woman, and blew up the pirate, is that correct?"

"That's correct, Captain," I said. "We have no quarrel with you or the Bahamas. Surely, you can have none with us for hunting down a pirate."

"If she was a pirate, Captain, you are right that we have no need to quarrel," he answered. "I suspect she was since the other boaters saw a Jolly Roger flying from her. Some of them thought you were a pair of movie ships until I pointed out the absence of cameras and the very real way in which you two fought. Certainly, none of those you killed got up again. In fact, they were still on the ship when it blew up. No, sir, I have no reason to doubt you. However, there does seem to be something *odd* about all of this."

"I concur, Captain," I replied, still wondering, among other things, what a movie ship and cameras were, as well as why dead men would get up again. It was then that Mr. Newton interrupted with his damage report, and when he finished, I asked the Bahamian Captain, "Well, then am I correct, sir, that Nassau is nearby? We'll need to lay over long enough to make repairs before we return to Boston. As well as the fight, we had to sail through a bad storm."

"Yes, Nassau is nearby, Captain, but we would prefer that you drop anchor here and wait until another American ship arrives. We've taken the liberty to call in the American Navy because of the American flag you're flying, and because we feel they are better able to handle this situation. Will you do as we ask?"

"We will, sir," I answered, finding the phrase *called in* as baffling as the other oddities, while wondering how long we would have to wait, especially since even a ship dispatched from Charleston, South Carolina would take many hours, even a day, to reach our current position. "What should we do in the event of bad weather?"

"In that event, we'll escort you to Nassau, sir," he replied although he seemed to think such a thing would be unnecessary.

I then had Mr. Jenkins see to the anchor, while I instructed the men in our nests to watch for the arrival of another ship, and for any adverse weather that would require ending our anchorage. I further ordered that we make what repairs we could, and that we keep our colors aloft for the time being. Then I noticed Miss Walton's concerned look.

"I must confess that this is all just as peculiar to me," I said in an aside. "Something odd has happened, to be sure."

"Well, there must be a logical explanation for these strange boats and all the other oddities, Captain. You're right something peculiar has happened to us, and since I was on *Graywolf,* that would suggest that the same thing happened to the pirate as well. No, if you ask me, it's as if we're out of place, Captain Dawes."

"Interesting phrase, with a fair deal of merit to it. Allow me to suggest that we see what the balance of the day brings. Then, at dinner, you, my officers and myself will try to further assess things, while I'll have Tibbs gather thoughts from the crew, which he will then bring before us. Perhaps, one of the men saw something that would help us."

"I like your plan," she said with a nod. "I also must admit that I like how you treat your crew, both officer and man, and if their sharpness is a result of that, then I am still more impressed."

"Thank you," I replied, wondering if had misjudged her. Learning more about Miss Walton might confirm that, and so I asked, "Well, is there anything you wish to tell me about the pirates or your captivity?"

"There's not much to tell," Miss Walton answered. "I was locked up in a small cabin near the main cabin, and I had no idea of what was happening, beyond the passage of two nights and the storm we went through. Then, as we left the storm behind, I heard the pirates start to shout about you, and not long after that, I heard cannon fire followed by something heavy falling on the quarterdeck. There was a new barrage of cannon fire, and it sounded like Captain Barber's cabin exploded. A great deal of shouting followed, and finally the Captain came and pulled me out into his room. We stood at the door to the main deck, and when we could no longer hear any sounds of fighting, he opened the doors and brought me out as you saw."

"Well, it is always interesting to hear things from a different perspective," I concluded. "Certainly, yours has been a dreadful lot, Miss Walton, but the worst is over, and you seem to be unharmed."

"I am, thanks to you and your gallant ship, Captain Dawes. Yet, my wonder at where we are makes me also sense that things aren't really over for those of us on this ship. No, until we see Boston or one of the other American ports, I'll maintain that stance."

"That's very sensible. At the same time, my prevailing sense is that none of us is in great physical jeopardy. That is, there's nothing like *Graywolf* threatening us," I observed.

"Yes, that is so. I also see where your notion is correct—we *should* wait and see what develops. I always admire a man with a wealth of patience."

"Why, thank you," I said and nodded. "Most seamen are like that. It's a necessary trait, borne of long journeys."

"Well put, Captain. Perhaps, though, it is best to say that most *American* seamen are patient!" she corrected. "Captain Webster of *HMS Bennett* was hardly patient. I could tell that from just watching him from the deck of *Seacastle*. I especially did not care for the way he treated his men, and because of that, I was glad to not be on his ship."

"Was he fairly exacting and demeaning toward them?"

"Yes. How did you know?"

"Unfortunately, that is the way of most British Navy Captains. To my mind, it is a hidden advantage for us. Tell me, who will win at Chess, the dull-witted man who is little more than a beast of burden, or the sharp-witted sailor like Tibbs, up there, who not only sees far, but can quickly assess what he sees?"

"Why, your man Tibbs, of course!"

"That's what I mean. So, tell me, did you learn the first name of this Captain Webster?"

"William, I believe."

"Slightly older than myself?"

"You know him, don't you?"

"I do, and if you will allow, I will amuse you by telling you how, which will also tell you quite a bit about this ship."

"Why, I would be most interested in learning *all* that I can about *Scorpion*. If nothing else, that will give me still more to report to Uncle."

"It certainly will."

Clearly, I still found her intriguing, despite my thoughts on our differences. Miss Walton was a wonderfully sensible, young woman. Too many of the ones I had known had been dull-witted, boring creatures, little more than live dolls. Yet, Lord Cornwallis's niece was well schooled in sound reasoning and in carrying on a good conversation. I admired her for that, even more than for her pleasant looks, which were framed by dark curls that were beginning to lose their shape. Then there was her unstated courage that had given her the sand to travel the Atlantic alone.

Yet, the specter of our differences rose anew to beat down my interests. Despite her dismay about the treatment of the sailors on *HMS Bennett,* she likely had no reason to think ill of the divisions and other wedges that ran like a garden rampant through English society. I, however, had every reason to abhor them. At the same time, I had to remain polite. Then, before I could begin to tell her about my ship, I remembered the first rule with ladies, regardless of age or courage.

"Seaman Garber!"

"Aye, sir!"

"Would you see to bringing a bench on deck for Miss Walton."

"Aye, sir! Won't be long at it, miss," he added, touching his brow to her.

Smiling graciously, she said, "Thank you, Seaman Garber. Thank you, Captain Dawes."

"Of course," I replied, before I briefly told her William Webster's connection to *Scorpion.*

Laughing, she admitted, "I think he would be furious to know the truth in this matter."

"No doubt," I agreed. Then, turning back to the Bahamian boat and its Captain, I decided to try some diplomacy with him to ease the tension, and I asked, "Captain, would you and your crew like to come aboard?"

"No, thank you, sir. I appreciate your offer, but we must receive permission from our commander before we go aboard a foreign vessel."

"Very well, Captain," I answered. "Yes, I think it would be best to leave things as they are until the other American ship arrives."

"That was my hope as well," he answered. "I will, however, make a note in my log that you never acted in a hostile manner toward us. I appreciate that."

"Well, I've always believed in being cordial to all of those I meet. There's little merit in bickering, and none at all in insults or coming to blows."

"Truly," he said with admiration. Then he noted, "Well, I am Captain John Clayton."

"Captain Sam Dawes," I answered before we exchanged salutes. "Pleasure to meet you, John, " I said, hoping we could get beyond his subservient formality.

"Likewise...sir," he responded.

"Call me Sam, Captain," I urged.

"Thank you, Sam."

"So, John, what material was used in making your speaking trumpet?"

"Why, this is plastic," he replied with a slight frown.

"And your boat?"

"Fiberglass," he answered, frowning anew.

John was about to ask me something, when Tibbs rather excitedly cried, "Captain!—ship approaching!—off the port bow!"

✳✳✳

OF COURSE, JUST then, none of us on deck could see the object of Tibbs's excitement. I knew from my visits to that crow's nest that the approaching ship could be far away. Yet, knowing it was Tibbs, a man not given to excess or wild imaginings, we all felt inclined to wait, even Miss Walton who nodded at my assurances about Tibbs. Moments later, other men aloft were also beginning to point and cry out, some with great disbelief. However, I decided to remain where I was—to maintain an example of calm. Miss Walton was there, and my new friend, Captain John Clayton, still hovered nearby while he remained on the bow of his boat. The latter was somewhat dismayed by those initial outcries of my crew.

In the meantime, Garber returned with the requested seat and set it where Miss Walton indicated. As it was, our wait was twice interrupted on that most unusual day. Initially, the first of those disruptions added further seeds to our bewilderment although all of us have come to better understand both. However, just then, those seeds of understanding lacked the proper nurturing to make them sprout. The nurturing was also about to begin.

The young woman again thanked both the seaman and myself, before she settled on her perch with a smile as she observed, "I had no idea that you Rebels could be so genteel. Father thought you had all become no better than the red savages that frequent the Colonies and the New World. Well, as it happened, Uncle's letters to my mother put things quite differently, while they also painted an intriguing picture of America. So, I decided to come and see for myself. Tell me, Captain, do you agree with my father that it is foolish for a young woman to travel to America on her own?"

"Not at all. This war is about freedom. We want ours from England, while we also want to establish a society free from classes and other distinctions," I concluded, realizing too late that I had led us headlong into the topic of division.

"Oh? Interesting."

"Why, my friend Thomas Jefferson thinks we could work things out so that there are no divisions between men and women, or between whites, blacks and Native Americans," I continued, deciding it was better to go forward with the topic than retreat from it. "Only by living that way will we know true peace and harmony, and be strong enough to defend our nation. Still, my point is that while such ideals have yet to be realized, there are minds at work in this nation that say they should be. Jefferson is not alone there."

"I imagine not. Certainly, he must have the support of many in Congress."

"No doubt he does, but I'm not sure that he has the support of the majority, while even if he did, Congress would likely wait on such things until our independence is secured. At the same time, as an intelligent young woman that means that there is an enormous potential for you in this land, which has yet to realize its own potential, and that is why I think you're right to come to America, regardless of the circumstances."

"Why, still another interesting point," she mused.

"Well, I'm glad to learn of your fascination. However, I feel I must correct one of your impressions. Most of the Native Americans are no more savage than you or I. They may live in a manner far different from ours, and while there is a brutal nature to their warfare, those I have met have a wonderful sort of nobility about them. Further, the older ones are often more than willing to honor you with the wisdom they have gained. No, Miss Walton, I feel we ought to make every effort to include the natives in our society, or to at least learn how not to interfere with theirs."

Some people might have recoiled in outrage at such brash words. Others would be so incensed at my equating our red brothers with ourselves that they would have turned on their heels and walked away. Yet, the young woman before me was ever the picture of consideration and care.

"Why, what an interesting revelation, Captain," she replied, more intrigued than angered.

Just then, a loud, popping noise marked the start of the first intrusion. When my guest paused and looked toward the top of our foremast as she sought the source of the noisy flop-flop sound, I followed Miss Walton's glance and noted the gray, oblong device, which had a bow that was half glass and a stern that looked like a tapering horizontal spar. Two men in helmets were visible through the glass in the bow, and black letters on the sides of the craft spelled out *US NAVY*. I looked at my passenger as the airship made a long circle of *Scorpion*. It now seemed clear to me why things had taken on such an odd sheen.

"It appears, Miss Walton, that *Scorpion* somehow chased you and *Graywolf* into the future."

"I tend to agree. Certainly, this flying machine is unlike anything our present had. Perhaps, Captain Clayton can tell us more," she suggested.

"I imagine he can," I said with a nod and went to the rail. "John? What can you tell us about this airship?"

The black man frowned and said, "Tell you? Well, Sam, it's a helicopter. Tell me, what year do you think this is?"

"For us, it should be seventeen seventy-seven." He gaped, and I added, "That's not correct, is it? This is the future. At least, it is to us. Is that right, John?"

"By more than two centuries. How that is, I couldn't say, but at the same time I feel compelled to believe you. That fight you put on with the other ship was real. So were those men you killed to rescue the young lady. What's more, I deem you're far too honest to make up such a thing."

"Well, thank you, for believing in us. So, tell me, John, how does this helicopter fly? I see no wings like a bird's."

"Well, over the top are large, horizontal blades that spin very fast and act like wings. They make the thumping noise you hear. Then, there's smaller vertical blades off the tail that stabilize and steer the helicopter."

He looked up suddenly, and following his glance, we saw a second helicopter come into view. This one was red and white, and had the letters *ABC* on its side. In addition to the two-person crew, it carried a pair of passengers.

"Oh-oh!—now *everyone* will know about you!"

As I wondered what he meant, I focused on the four people in this helicopter. Again, the helmeted pair in the forward cabin were concerned with the operation of the machine. The other two were a man and woman in the aft cabin who were readily visible because the door on that side of the ship had been slid open. The man held a black oblong device on his shoulder that ended with a lensed tube. The woman leaned out beside him as she talked into an upright stick in her hand.

"What's that black tube with the lens, a modern long glass?" I asked.

"It's a television camera, Captain. It won't harm you or your ship, but by it, many people will get to see both, even though they're not here."

Before I could wonder aloud about that, a commotion erupted on our bow as several of my men rushed forward to observe the approach of the ship Tibbs had sighted.

⌘⌘⌘

Chapter VII

A MEETING

IT WAS AS amazed as every man and officer of my crew by the sight of our modern counterpart. Miss Walton openly gaped at the vessel that drew along side. Two centuries of progress had greatly transformed warships. Gone were two or more masts straining with wind-filled canvas. Absent were rows of cannon poking their muzzles through ports in the sides. Missing was the web of lines and a bell for sounding the hour or signaling the crew into general quarters. I was not as surprised as some. After all, it was logical to assume that if engines could make helicopters fly, they could also make ships move without the aid of wind. Other refinements or changes seemed to concur with the premise of some two hundred years of improvements. Yet, did they necessarily make *Scorpion* obsolete?

As for improvements—or changes, if you prefer—we saw a single mast affixed to the rear of the glass-fronted chamber that held the helm. That wheelhouse was positioned on the forward end of a long cabin that was positioned atop the middle third of the main deck. After the pilothouse, came a vertical tube that emitted a vapor from within, and then a flat space that was the resting place for the helicopter, which was just then winding down from its flight. I regretted not seeing it land, but sensed that that action would soon become commonplace to Miss Walton, my crew, and myself. Then, on either end of the ship, was an enclosed single-barrel cannon that was presently turned toward us. Pivoting also appeared to be possible with each of the artificial trees with arrow-like devices for branches that stood between the cannon and main cabin. Her name was *John Paul Jones* and her class was frigate. The name was vaguely familiar to me. I thought he was the master of another privateer, and I remembered talk about acquiring a frigate from France to act as a raider. Was there a connection? I sensed I would learn that as well.

After letting everyone get a good look, I called the crew into formation, handed it over to Mr. Jenkins, and went to the port rail with my trumpet in hand. By then, the frigate had pulled alongside. Her crewmembers, uniformed in beige or various shades of blue, filled many of her railings. On seeing me, each group was called to attention by an officer who saluted me for them. I returned each salute, to include the one from their captain who came out of the wheelhouse with his gray trumpet.

The latter inquired, "Who are you?"

"*Scorpion*, United States Navy."

"Homeport?"

"Boston. Would you like to come aboard?"

Smiling with understanding and appreciation, he replied, "Be there shortly."

I then watched as a derrick behind the helicopter was used to lower a small boat and its crew. The hoist likely had a motor of its own since it didn't rely on a system of humans and pulleys. The Captain was waiting at the foot of the stairs siding the ship by the time the launch reached that point. Then he sharply stood the bow all the while that the boat brought him over to *Scorpion*. As best I could tell, the man at the stern of the boat not only operated its rudder, but also was in charge of the engine that propelled the vessel. Apparently, oars were also no long employed by the modern Navy. It made me wonder why there was a need for such a large crew if machines did everything.

After scaling our rope ladder and alighting on the deck, the Captain saluted me and asked, "Permission to come aboard."

"Granted, Captain," I said. Then extending my hand, I added, "I'm Sam Dawes, Captain of *Scorpion*. Welcome aboard."

"Commander Greg Brosky, Captain of *John Paul Jones*. What's your primary duty out of Boston, Sam?" he asked, after his eyes had fondly assessed the spars and rigging above us.

"We're serving as a privateer, operating under the authority of the Second Continental Congress. Our most recent mission was hunting down a pirate named *Graywolf* that had abducted a passenger from a merchantman. The passenger in question is the young woman there, Miss Deborah Walton, a niece of the British general, Lord Cornwallis."

"Lord Cornwallis?" he wondered with interest as if he recognized the name.

After nodding, I said, "That's right. However, Greg, I understand from having talked to Captain Clayton of the Bahamas that our present is now the past. How that happened, I'm not certain. Perhaps, the storm we passed through had something to do with it. After all, *Graywolf* was transported through time as well. Yet, before I formally announce anything to my crew, I feel it would be best to confer with you in my cabin."

"I think you're right, Sam. Still, I think we can take a few minutes to review your crew."

"Very good. Please keep in mind that we had action less than two hours ago. That may account for the appearance of some of them, especially since we had just finished our clean up when you came along. As it is, we have repairs that can only be made while in port."

"Sure, I'll keep that in mind," Captain Brosky said with a nod.

He had a wonderfully warm way of looking over my men. Every so often, he would stop before one of them, ask the man his name and primary duties, find something to compliment, and then move on to the next. Indeed, it was much the same way I reviewed them, and from that, I saw where, perhaps, some things had not changed. Then, after he had briefly met Miss Walton, who glowed with womanly interest for him, Greg asked me to show him to my cabin.

Then, after I had left instructions for my crew to continue their duties, we went below.

✳✳✳

AVING TO CONFRONT adverse weather on a regular basis, a sailor quickly learns that there is little that can be done, beyond accepting its presence in his or her adventures on the sea, and beyond, of course, making the ship ready for such weather. Indeed, it is as much a part of those journeys, as following the determined course. Then, as has been noted earlier, the seafarer must learn how to survive and cope with such weather, but I think accepting it as part of the job makes coping and survival that much easier. In short, the mariner learns to accept all intrusions in life, while maintaining the course he or she has set. At least, the active sailor does. Those no longer active may forget how to do as much, to his or her detriment.

Of course, on a wind-powered ship like *Scorpion*, those stormy disruptions are still more trying. Yet, as has been observed, there is also the added comfort of having many shipmates about, since it is far better to confront a situation in the company of associates than to face it alone. It is still another reason to develop a sense of unity in the crew.

I knew that to be the case then—that my crew was ready to face adversity together in any guise, and even though none of us had openly discussed what had transpired as we chased *Graywolf* into the storm, I knew every crewman had already accepted whatever destiny that storm brought us, even if he didn't entirely understand it. That we would face our fate together was enough for all of us. However, now that our primary task, rescuing Miss Walton, had been completed, I, like my men, had no idea of how we were to proceed, in light of the staggering result of our fateful storm. Certainly, all of us had seen the flying ships, as well as *John Paul Jones*, and those observations were enough to prepare my crew for the formal announcement that was apt to follow my meeting with Captain Brosky. Further, given that, there was the somewhat more disturbing question of where we were to go that was beginning to loom over the horizon.

Consider that for a moment. Have you ever been faced with a situation like that? Have you ever been so lost that you had no idea of where home was? Or perhaps, like us, you knew where your home was, but you had no idea of how to physically reach it? Somewhere on this broad planet, each of you can settle into a nice chair near a warm fire, amid the glowing hugs and kindness of those you love. For many of you, such a thing can be achieved at the end of each day with a routine trip. For us, that was no longer possible. At least, we could no longer reach the homes that had been our present. So, where would our homes be in our new present? That was something I hoped would be answered by my private chat with Captain Brosky.

There was also my wonder of what would become of us. Could we find a use in the modern Navy? Could we adapt enough to our new society? Could we overcome an accident of fate that had cut us off from our old one? How would we manage and survive in our new present? Again, I sensed that the frigate's Captain would suggest something on that aspect.

As we entered the large aft cabin that had been the site of so many of my conversations with Captain Whyte and the various American radicals, I considered my counterpart. His grip was firm and confident. Yet, I think it was his ever-present grin that I found most favorable. He was truly happy to be doing what he did. He loved the sea, a good ship, and a good crew as much as I did. Yet, he was no less fervent about the United States. It was no wonder to me that we became good friends.

"Okay, Sam, why don't we sit at your table, while you tell me the details of all that's happened since you left Boston?"

"In a moment, Greg," I deferred. Then, as I motioned for *John Paul Jones*'s skipper to take a seat, I called through the door, "Steward!"

"Yes, sir!" Joe Greenwich, a black man of modest size but abundant strength, responded with his customary quickness.

"Joe, would you please bring coffee for Captain Brosky and myself?" I asked.

"Right away, sir. Welcome to *Scorpion*, Captain Brosky! Fine ship you have."

"Why, thank you, Joe."

The coffee arrived as I was telling Greg about our initial encounter with *Graywolf*. I kept my tale brief and to the point, and I ended it a few minutes later with the scuttling of the pirate. What my listener really wanted was a sense of what had happened there in the Bahamas, and how it had transpired. The Board of Inquiry, if there was one, could be as pointed as they so desired. They, after all, had to rule on what was the truth in the matter. Captain Brosky, on the other hand, wanted no more than an outline, so he could relay that information to his superior. It also was for him to judge whether something seriously improper had occurred. If he felt our actions were that improper, he could impound the ship and place all of us in the brig until we reached their homeport of Norfolk, Virginia.

"No, you were right to destroy *Graywolf*," Captain Brosky admitted. "Certainly, all of your actions were done in accordance with standard operating procedures from your present. Captain Clayton is right that a pirate is fair game for all warships, even in our time. Still, I suspect that even had you known where you really were, you wouldn't've done things different if only because you'd have no way of knowing how we operate. Why, as incredible as all this is, I also have no trouble believing you. It's not hard for me to see that you're honest, and that this ship is authentic."

"Thank you, Greg. Are there those who might not believe the truth in this matter?"

"If there are, Sam, we can give them all sorts of evidence to support your account. Not only evidence of the battle you just fought, but also that you are, indeed, from 1777. One thing would be to instruct all of your men and Miss Walton to hold on to all of their money and valuables. Those alone will help to date you and the ship."

"Why, then the same would be true of the contents of the chest there," I observed. "It contains pirate loot from *Graywolf*."

"Well, not only would that help prove your authenticity, it would also provide financial security for all of you. That loot, Sam, is bound to be worth a substantial amount of money, and right now, our laws recognize all of you as the lawful owners. As for your action with the pirate," Greg continued, "we can start with the hundreds of people who saw your battle, and then we can get divers to salvage things from *Graywolf*. Beyond that, I couldn't say, but we could figure something out. No, I think the main question confronting us now is *what* to do with you. We don't have the means or the technology to return you to 1777. Yet, I do believe we can learn much from you."

"We will be glad to reveal all that we can," I noted, beginning to sense that our new culture would somehow find a way to accommodate us. "However, I am most certain that the intrigue of being a living museum will be short-lived, and that we will need a more useful function in this society to sustain us. I include the ship, as well as my crew and myself in that vision."

"I can well appreciate your concern, Sam. Believe me, I'll see that it gets every consideration. For now, while we sail to Nassau, I'd like us to confer with Miss Walton and your officers. Only after that will we formally tell your crew what's happened."

I nodded, and we sent Joe topside with instructions, to include setting sail for Nassau, in conjunction with the frigate.

✳✳✳

THE THING ABOUT storms, of course, is that you almost always can anticipate their coming into your life. Perhaps, if you're distracted by a gull until the black clouds are sweeping over you, you won't see the storm soon enough to prepare for it. Otherwise, the dark sky, the rise of the wind, the sudden chill in the air, even a distant report of thunder, all of these serve to herald the storm, and so, we are able to make ready. We had even been able to prepare for our two encounters with *Graywolf*, just as we had been able to prepare for her destruction.

Yet, there was no way we could prepare for the act of travelling through Time, even though we still had to accept the fact that we *had*. How can you *not* accept the reality of what has happened to you? Perhaps, though, our learning to accept storms, and to otherwise be resilient, allowed us to bravely confront those challenges that came without the slightest warning. Miss Walton, on the other hand, did not have that advantage, and that lack of experience had made her more concerned. Yet, it was my belief that her innate courage had clearly minimized that concern, so that it only manifested itself in a wavering smile and a mild darting quality in her green eyes.

SCORPION—*James R. Poyner*

Captain Brosky and I properly stood as the young woman entered my cabin in the company of my officers. When she had been seated at the foot of the table, Greg and I resumed our seats leaving Jenkins, Newton and Third Mate Carter to fill in the other spaces. The latter were only a little surprised to learn of our fate since they had been sharing their own speculations, while my words served to confirm what Miss Walton and I had begun to suspect.

"No, sir," Jenkins said as the senior officer of the three, "we worked out the same conclusion after seeing the airships. I wouldn't be surprised, as you suspect, if some—if not most—of the men, particularly Tibbs, have also guessed the truth in this matter, as well. Still, we agree that the entire crew should be told. This ship has always been operated in an honest and straightforward manner, and this would be a poor occasion to abandon that policy."

"A most valid point, Lieutenant," I noted. "Miss Walton?"

"I think that is the fairest approach, Captain Dawes. As for myself, I do appreciate being told the truth in this situation. It is hard to say whether or not it is a pity that we cannot return home. For some of your crew with families, it will be a hard blow, and you must be prepared to help those men."

"She's right there, Sam," Greg said.

"Well, none of us were married," I answered. "A few had sweethearts in Boston, and they will likely be saddened to learn the truth. Still, I'm sure we can identify those individuals and be ready to help them. The rest of us will stoically accept this as a consequence of the storm"

"That is the best approach," Captain Brosky said with a nod of admiration. "So, what good do you see in this accident of fate, Miss Walton?"

Properly, the young woman took a moment to arrive at a thoughtful response, and then she replied, "Well, Captain, I can see where this promises to be a wonderful new society for us. Ships that fly, small boats that move gracefully over the water, great naval vessels that are sleek and trim, all of these make me curious to see and learn more. Indeed, having noticed young women on your ship and one in one of the airships, I sense that women presently have a much more equal role, and that also interests me. I suppose the only question that remains for me is what happened to my uncle, Lord Charles Cornwallis, and to England in the war? Your ship, Captain Brosky, is evidence that we either lost, or that we eventually gave America her freedom."

"Well, when the French, as allies of the United States, mastered the British Navy, your uncle was pinned down at Yorktown and was forced to surrender to George Washington," Greg explained with a crisp precision. "As it happened, that was the final action of the Revolution, and it ensured American independence.

"Oh, my!—poor uncle!" Miss Walton sighed as though she had somehow failed in a pursuit. "Well, then what is the relationship between the United States and Britain today?"

"We are the best of friends," he answered.

"Well, perhaps what happened to *Scorpion* was *meant* to happen," Miss Walton suggested. Then she sighed anew, "But, ohh, poor Uncle!"

We were about to console her, when one of my lads appeared in the doorway and cried, "Captain, one of the small boats has pulled alongside, and a man on it said he wants to talk to you."

While there was only a mild urgency in Draper's voice, we all followed him topside at a good pace. Naturally, I led the way. Whatever problem was the cause for my man's concern was meant for me to see first. That was the way of all ships. The commander of each one has the ultimate responsibility for his charge. He has to account for its safety and performance. He is the one all eyes turn to whenever a question arises regarding that ship. That is why the Captain is the focal point of a Board of Inquiry. It is why he is praised or blamed for his ship's actions. Captain Brosky understood and appreciated that role enough to let me take and maintain the lead. Another lad waved us over to the port rail just forward of the mizzen ratline.

"Thank you, Warner," I said as I reached him and looked over the side.

One of the small boats had indeed come alongside and, like the others, was easily keeping pace with us. I was no longer surprised by that, nor by what I did see. Remember, as a seasoned man of the sea, I had learned to accept all intrusions as a part of fate. If nothing else, I knew that there was nothing I could do to prevent them from happening. At best, I could deal with them in the appropriate manner.

A man clad only in what you call swimming trunks stood on the bow of that boat and, spying me, called, "Captain, can we come on board?"

It was a question based on curiosity as much as anything. It was also one that I had never entirely expected. My first thoughts were two-sided. On the one hand, I wanted to be as amenable as possible. On the other, we were conducting operations as a ship of the United States Navy, and even in our day, it had been unheard of for civilians to come on board a warship for a tour when that ship was not docked at a pier. Guessing that that policy still remained, I conferred briefly with Greg.

Then, I told the man, "We'll gladly welcome all of you aboard when we've docked in Nassau!"

"Then we'll see you there, Captain!" he answered and waved to the others to join him in speeding off to our destination.

As the boaters hurried off, Captain Brosky once more assured me that it was normal for a Navy ship to hold tours while in port, and that, as long as the Navy did not quash the idea when he made his report, he saw no reason to keep us from doing as much.

⌘⌘⌘

Chapter VIII

AT PORT

ENSING THAT THERE would be many others interested in touring *Scorpion*, I coordinated efforts to prepare for them, with Captain Brosky serving as a most able advisor. A plan was worked up for the route of the tour, and all of my officers were familiarized with it since they would act as the guides. We also set up the teams of seamen who would be stationed at each point of interest, ready to perform and explain a related task. Greg liked that, while Miss Walton smiled at our resourcefulness. As the tours were rehearsed, the Captain and I took her aside.

"What would you prefer, Miss Walton?" I asked. "There is a spare cabin below in this ship that could accommodate you and a female officer from the Captain's ship, or he will have his launch take you over to *John Paul Jones*, where you'll reside until we've reached Norfolk."

"Either way," Captain Brosky said, "Ensign Johnson should be able to help you adjust to your new society."

"Well, I think it might be best if I go over to your ship, Captain Brosky. I feel I could learn much more about our new society by sailing with you. What's more, I could pass on the pertinent aspects of that knowledge to Captain Dawes and his crew," she concluded although I sensed that she also wished to be on *John Paul Jones* because Greg would be on it.

I had no regrets there. Her interest in me had never been as apparent as that she held for Greg. Further, the latter seemed just as fascinated with the young woman. With little delay, we agreed with her choice, and before long, Lord Cornwallis's niece was on her way to the frigate. I had no regrets for that either. Again, there was no romantic interest between us, while our different histories and backgrounds might have made it difficult to be friends. At least, she did not seem as willing to bridge that difference as Tibbs. What was more, my emerging friendship with Greg was enough to let me honor any promising romantic interest between Miss Walton and him.

Yet, what we hadn't anticipated was the small boats serving as heralds of our arrival at Nassau.

✳✳✳

THE JUBILATION THAT greeted us, as we at last turned into the port, was a wonderful testament to how quickly news travels in our new present. That we *were* the news was an unfamiliar role for the ship and crew, as well as myself. That it was us, who our greeters had turned out to see and honor, could easily have made all of us feel very uncomfortable, if not very much out of place. Instead, we each knew a pride in our ship and our new society. Otherwise, I had wisely begun our preparation by assembling the crew and telling them what had happened to us, and that, coupled with Greg assuring all of us through me that a useful role would be found for *Scorpion*, counteracted any sense of isolation from our new society. Those few men who had left behind sweethearts each reasoned out loud that that it was meant to be, and that it was better to simply accept it rather than challenge the Maker's methods. Of course, involving everyone in the crew in tour rehearsals and preparations also gave the crew something to do until we docked.

Then, at the entrance to the harbor, a great flotilla of small boats met and escorted us to our berth. They tooted their many horns, rang dozens of bells, and otherwise joyously welcomed us with celebration. What I had learned about Sir Francis Drake and the Spanish explorers briefly flashed into my mind—in that their tall ships had often been greeted in such a way. Yet, it was a moving sight for all of us, especially since many of the boaters marked their hurrahs by waving small American flags.

If nothing else, the spectacle made us feel welcome in our new society and further defeated any feelings of being alone in a new world, while doing a wonderful job of countering any regrets for what we had left behind. Yet, it also made us all feel like what you call celebrities, which, in turn, gave us a new sense of duty. We knew from Captain Brosky that it meant that many would look at us not only as heroes, but as role models—as people to *emulate*—and so, we had to set excellent examples for all of those that we met. Yet, even that was met as nothing more than a new challenge. Otherwise, from our days as a mail packet, my men and myself were well schooled in being hospitable to all visitors, which made it second nature for us to present our best image to everyone we encountered.

Before long, we had tied up to our pier and had begun to set in motion our plans for welcoming people to *Scorpion*. Thanks to our rehearsals, initiating that welcome went very smoothly, and we were confident the actual tours would as well. Captain Brosky had no objections to such proceedings. Ship tours, he reminded me once more, were to be expected. Further, they were the best way to honor a heroic, fighting ship. He did, however, ask me to confine my crew to the ship and the immediate area of the pier. He felt that

that might be best until the Navy had formally issued orders covering us.

Then he had his own quartermaster come aboard *Scorpion*, learn what we needed to make our repairs, and then the quartermaster saw that those items were promptly brought to our ship, along with the goods Joe had requested for the galley.

✳✳✳

DURING THOSE FIRST hours of our arrival in Nassau on that most eventful day, the services of Greg's quartermaster proved most useful since it allowed us to commence the more involved repairs with little delay, as well as replenish our stores of food. I assigned a half dozen men to make the repairs, those taking part in the tours already had their tasks, while I had the balance of the crew standing by to lend a hand as needed. We did modify our tours to include explanatory stops before or below the repairmen, and to show how the hoist was used to lower our fruits and other fare into the hold. Otherwise, my job was to welcome people as they left the gangplank for the main deck. Tibbs and my three officers were each teamed with two seamen, and each trio would take a dozen or so visitors on a walk through the ship.

The most fascinating stop for most people was the one that let them watch our top two gun crews race each other in preparing and firing their cannon. Other men would demonstrate how they climbed the ratlines to the crow's nest on the mainmast, while still others furled and unfurled the royal yard on the foremast. Other demonstrations revolved around working the windlass, manning the helm, Joe demonstrating how meals were cooked on the ship, and a good look at my cabin, with our chart for the Bahamas on display. Then, as each tour group returned to me, I would take a few minutes to respond to any questions.

One lad asked, "Is it true that you sank a pirate ship today?"

"True, indeed, lad," I nodded.

"Boy, that musta been *neat!"* he thrilled.

When his parents partially frowned, I noted, "No, lad, killing other men is not something to be enjoyed as though it were a game. Life is the most *precious* gift the Creator has given us, and any life lost is something to be regretted. Yet, we are always faced with circumstances that may lead to killing others. Our pursuit of *Graywolf* in order to rescue Miss Walton was just such a circumstance. Tomorrow a new circumstance may arise and take us far from here. Yet, there isn't a man on this ship who doesn't hope that that tomorrow and that circumstance will *never* come. We all want perpetual peace and harmony."

Even though several adults in his group applauded my words, the lad still asked, "Then why do men cheer when they win a fight?"

"Good question," I said with a knowing smile. "Well, we cheer because each victory against villains, like pirates and ruthless tyrants, brings us that much closer to that very day of true peace and harmony that we seek for the world. Yet, until those servants of evil are all dispatched, there will always be a need for *brave* men and women to fight them." A thoughtful quiet from the adults in the crowd prompted me to cup the shoulder of the young fellow, as I added, "Remember that, will you, lad?"

"Aye-aye, Captain!" he replied with an enthusiasm and a salute that reminded me of our cabin boy Bart, who had returned to England and his parents from Calcutta.

After returning his salute, I then watched Bart's modern apparition lead his parents from the ship, and I was quick to note the young woman from the ABC helicopter and her cameraman hovering nearby. They had come on board moments before, conferred with Captain Brosky, and all three had heard the conclusion of my remarks to the young lad and his group. The woman's smile, in the wake of those words, not only told me that she had heard them, but that she also liked them. Then, after a moment, Greg brought them up to me.

He at once explained, "Captain Dawes, this is Anita Blake from the American Broadcasting Company." We shook hands as we cordially greeted each other, while Commander Brosky added, "ABC is one of our country's news-dispensing companies."

"Do you mean, Greg, that her company is something like a newspaper, but that it uses this gentleman's device and her stick to somehow present the news?"

"That's it, Sam," the Captain nodded. "I'll explain better another time."

"Yes, that is fair. We shouldn't keep Miss Blake and her man...Uh, what is your name, sir?"

"Bill Dakota, Captain," the cameraman noted, shooting out his hand.

As we shook hands, I marveled at his strength and noted, "Welcome. Do I correctly judge that you're a Native American, Bill?"

"Full-blooded Dakota, Captain."

"Dakota? If memory serves they were in the nether regions of the Great Lakes, near Lake Superior."

"They were. I'm from South Dakota and the Black Hills—that's a good way west of the Mississippi," he added. When I nodded, Bill concluded, "Well, I do this because I like being among the first to see things like your ship. She's a beauty, sir."

"Well, thank you, Bill. Well, we shouldn't keep you and Miss Blake..."

"Anita will be fine, Captain," the young woman insisted.

"Well, thank you, Anita. Call me Sam, if you like," I said with a slight bow that also made her smile.

"Anita has some questions for you," Greg noted, "and then, they'd like a brief tour of your ship with you and one of your men. I see no harm in either."

"Then neither do I," I said. "If you would, Anita, allow me to name Seaman John Tibbs to be that man."

"Of course, Captain," she said, smiling again in appreciation for my manners as if they were something rare.

"Tibbs!" I called, waving him toward us.

"Aye, sir!" he returned, as he waited for a new tour group to form, and then, ever the model of self-confidence, shoulders back, power in his stride, he strode over to us.

"Anita, allow me to present Seaman John Tibbs who has been my shipmate for many years, and who is both the senior crewman and the watch for our foremast's crow's nest. He is the ship's eyes, just as I suspect Bill is the eyes for your news." When both of my visitors nodded at my perception, I added, "Tibbs, Miss Anita Blake and her cameraman, Bill Dakota."

"Welcome aboard, miss," he said, as they shook hands. "Welcome, Bill," he added and shook hands with the cameraman.

After they thanked him for the greetings, I said, "Tibbs, I'd like you to have your two lads take over my duties with the visitors, while you and I show these two the ship after we answer their questions."

"Aye, sir."

When Tibbs returned to us, I asked, "Now, how would you like to do this, Anita? Might I suggest that Tibbs work with Bill by directing him to the various features of the ship?"

"That would be best," she said with a nod, as Greg looked on with an appreciative grin. "Actually, for now, I'd like to ask you a few questions and have a brief look at *Scorpion*. Then I'd like to return with Bill some time in the near future for a more extensive interview and tour."

SCORPION—*James R. Poyner*

The whole idea came as an interesting proposal to me. Such a thing had never been tried in my day, but of course, sailing ships were so commonplace back then that there was little need to educate or inform the public about them. I also saw where Miss Blake and her organization could do much to introduce us to our new world in a way that would be very suitable, while we, in turn, would learn something from having to work with one of the more modern aspects of our new society.

"Are you sure it's all right, Greg?" I asked as my sense of duty rose to challenge the propriety of such a thing.

"Well, Sam," he began, "I see no harm in granting Anita's request since she's already told the world about you, from her helicopter, and since my superiors still haven't asked me to put a lid on any further reporting. That is, I haven't been ordered to restrain journalists from talking to you.

"I understand, Captain," I said. "All right, Anita, three questions for Tibbs, three for me, and a short tour for now. Then there will be something more extensive when it's convenient to both of us. Fair enough?"

"Sure, that's reasonable."

She then arranged for a live transmission. That involved using what she called a communication satellite, a man-made device that orbited the earth much like the moon. I was, of course, still more amazed by that. Tibbs answered her questions of him by saying it was an enjoyable pursuit, he always loved the far-flung view of things from the crow's nest, and like the other men, he held me in dear regard because I cared as much about them as I did about the ship. He added that, given a chance, he hoped to take her cameraman aloft when they came for their more extensive look. Bill admitted he was up to the challenge, while Anita agreed that it would be a most interesting perspective. She then proceeded to ask who I was, why *Scorpion* had engaged and sunk *Graywolf*, and what our immediate future was. I answered the first two with brevity and the third with Captain Brosky's hope for us.

With a wishful smile, Miss Blake responded to my last answer, as she said, "Ohh, I hope the Navy *can* find a useful place for all of you as well. Still, I think there will be many others interested in learning all they can about and from you. Historians, archeologists and even shipbuilders will likely come to see you, if only to satisfy their own curiosities with their own questions."

"I see your point," I said with a nod. "Certainly, we will accommodate those people as best we can." Finally, I looked at my counterpart and asked, "Well, Captain Brosky, would you be interested in joining us for our brief tour?"

"I would, Captain," Greg said with a smile.

"Lead the way, Captain Sam," Anita urged. "We can keep recording even after we lose the link-up."

I nodded, as I considered how fondly she had smiled at me the entire time, and how much I liked the appellation *Captain Sam.*

⌘⌘⌘

Chapter IX

A CALL TO DUTY

THE TROUBLE WITH being a warship is that the immediate fruits of your success can be short-lived. That is, tomorrow, even the next hour, can *demand* your return to sea, with little delay. When so summoned, we respond without question and serve our nation and society to the best of our abilities, and with all of our courage and strength, as well as all manner of experience. At times, of course, such wants aren't entirely welcome, especially when the ship is docked at a pleasant place like Nassau. All sailors love the sea, but we also love calling at a port that is blessed with liveliness, with good eateries, and with those who admire and appreciate sailors.

Indeed, at Nassau, we were blessed with excellent weather, a colorful port, and a setting that was endowed with a bounty of natural beauty. It was, indeed, a heady mixture, one that was filled with temptation. Yet, as nice as all that is, it is then that conscience and dedication to duty are ultimately tested. Failure of either by too many hands ends the effectiveness of the crew and, in turn, its ship. Failure of one ship to respond to a call to duty, on the other hand, can readily undermine her nation's needs, and even, threaten that nation's existence.

On *Scorpion*, there was the wonderful understanding that we could never trade our obligation to America for moments of pleasure, since the aspect of pleasure would vanish before the grim guilt of our conscience. That is, it is impossible to *truly* enjoy that which you know you should not be doing. Knowing that, to the man, we of *Scorpion* might sigh at orders that called us away from a paradise like Nassau, but in the next instant, we would turn to the tasks of weighing anchor, casting off all lines, and heading out to sea. What is more, we would go without questioning our orders, even if they sent us into ready danger.

Given that, it was fortunate that, by the next afternoon, our repairs were finished and that we had not been allowed to go beyond our pier. That time, while Mr. Jenkins oversaw the visitors' tours, I was to be ferried over to *John Paul Jones* for my first visit to a modern warship. I had wanted to take Tibbs, of course, but when it came time for me to go, the line of visitors had not abated enough to let us cut back to two tour groups.

"There'll be another chance, sir," he reminded me.

"Likely when we reach Norfolk, if not before," I noted.

"Soon enough for me, Captain. And then it'll be your turn to point things out to me, like I did that first time you came up to the nest," he added.

Trading fond grins, I replied, "Fair enough. See you in a bit then."

"Right, sir. Say hello to Miss Walton for me and the lads."

"Will do," I answered, and since I also intended to use that visit to *John Paul Jones* as a vehicle for gaining an understanding of the modern Navy and the ships of this time, as well as the era itself, I climbed down to the frigate's launch with a healthy interest.

"All set, sir?" the lad at the boat's helm asked.

"All set, Seaman Kravitz," I said, as I looked back with a smile, while I stood the bow, legs spread, hands together at the small of my back.

He and his mates glanced approvingly at each other, while the boat was directed toward its floating home. Clapping the shoulder of the nearest man, I then asked him to tell me about the more obvious features of his ship. He gladly explained that *John Paul Jones* was classed frigate and was armed with five-inch guns and Seahawk missiles, which were considered its offensive weapons, while it had smaller guns for defending against air attacks. Then he pointed out the various physical features. The room with the helm was known as the bridge. Behind it was the smokestack or funnel, which was the vent for the great machines that drove the ship's propellers. Motors, as I had guessed, worked the various derricks and were used to help precisely turn a turret or missile launcher. Range on both offensive systems was measured not in yards, but miles. Fighting at close range had also become old-fashioned.

"All very fascinating. So, Seaman Gray, do I guess correctly that your helicopter employs a similar, but smaller, machine to make it fly?"

"That's right, Captain," Seaman Gray said with a nod. "Those machines are all called engines. Sometimes they'll directly power a vehicle. The rest of the time, they generate electricity, which powers a device known as a motor. You'll see what I mean, the more you learn about us."

"I have no doubt I will." Then, as we drew near the stairway, I glanced at all of them and said, "Thanks, for bringing me over, lads. Each of you sets a fine example for the Navy."

With grins, they thanked me before Seaman Gray answered, "Our pleasure, sir. Truth is, most of us agree with Captain Brosky—there's something special about *Scorpion.* Maybe we need to be reminded of where we came from, but me and the guys think it's something more. It's just hard saying what it is."

"Well, likely that's what we call the spirit of the ship. Perhaps, I can arrange for all of you to spend a few days sailing with us. Then, if you like the experience, you could sign on with us. My guess is that all of you would make fine additions."

Again, they thanked me, before Seaman Gray added, "As for shipping out with you, the Navy usually reserves that for cadets, but maybe for you, they ought to make an exception. Working a rigged ship has to make every sailor a better sailor, whether he or she went to the academy or not. Well, go ahead. They're expecting you."

At the stairs' top, I saluted Lieutenant Commander Maris, the ship's Executive Officer, and then I asked, "Permission to come aboard, sir."

"Granted, sir. Welcome to *John Paul Jones*, Captain Dawes."

I thanked him and then shook hands with Captain Brosky who had come forward to greet me. Not long after that, we had reviewed a phalanx of his crew, which included a good smattering of women, all of those sailors in crisp white uniforms and shimmering black shoes, and then we began our tour. I was even more fascinated with all that I saw and heard during that jaunt. We started at the bridge, toured the communications room, which held their radios, radar, sonar and the other modern devices that enhanced detection and communication. There were no more crow's nests for Tibbs to rule, while he looked through the compass.

Then I was shown into the aft gun turret and marveled at how the piece was breech-loaded and that the powder came wrapped in silk pillows that followed the shell into the breech. Swabbing was still done after each firing since that was still the best way to remove sparks that could ignite an explosion. From there, we worked our way down to the bottom of the ship, where I got to see the monstrous engines that powered the two screws. The tour ended with a meal, which featured my first hamburger and fries, and a tasty drink called Coke, as the Captain and I exchanged views on our different ships.

"Oh, I agree with you, Sam, that my ship is faster," Captain Brosky said. "Yours, however, doesn't rely on fuel that can be exhausted."

"Well, we have been becalmed. We also can't sail *into* a wind, and compared to yours, our firepower is limited in range, as well as effectiveness. Given that, I believe we'd be a poor match for a modern ship."

"I'm not so sure about all that," he said to my surprise. "For one thing, I think *Scorpion* has some fight left in her. No, I'm going to recommend that we maintain *Scorpion* just as she is, leave you and most of your crew assigned to her, and fill out the crew with cadets, the more experienced of your men being assigned duties as trainers on our other training vessels." When I briefly frowned, he added, "Ohh, I'm sure they'll arrange to let you keep Tibbs. He's far too important to you and *Scorpion*. He's part of your ship's spirit, the embodiment of it, if you will."

"Well, I do hope the Navy will understand that," I said. "If not, they may understand that Tibbs and I agreed long ago that we would always be shipmates."

"Well, it wouldn't hurt to mention that to them. They do understand such things."

"At the same time, Greg, each of my crew has a great loyalty to the ship, the rest of the crew, and even myself. Maybe it would be better to add a score of hammocks to the forecastle, so we could simply serve as a training vessel. I also agree with one of your crewmen that seamen should get the chance to sail with us."

"You know, there's something to be said for all of that. I imagine women will want to sign on, as well."

"That would be no trouble. In our time, it was easy enough to accommodate them as passengers. It should be just as easy doing the same for those who want to crew with the ship," I added.

"Well, that sounds like the best possibility. Still another possibility would be to have you work in conjunction with the Coast Guard to help counteract smuggling. The sight of a ship with 5-inch guns that can hit a target miles away can be intimidating, but I personally think it's even more intimidating staring down the barrel of a loaded cannon. Well, at least, I'll pass those ideas onto my superiors once we clear the Board of Inquiry in Norfolk."

"As long as proper consideration is given to each man and officer, as well as the ship, we'd welcome any opportunity to serve the United States, Greg."

"I know you will, Sam. That's what I like about you and your men. You haven't lost sight of what comes first."

"Well, thank you, " I said. "So, what do you think will happen with the Board of Inquiry?" I then asked.

"Well, to tell the truth, I can't see it being more than a mere formality. After all, you acted properly in every respect, the only lives lost were those of the pirates, and you were operating under terms concurrent with your present. In other words, there's nothing for them to find wrong. At least, there isn't, as far as I can tell. What's more, there's something I think you should see that they're likely to see, if they haven't already."

"Oh? What's that?"

"C'mon, I'll show you," the Captain countered. Then he added, "This will also demonstrate what Anita does for a living."

"Well, then lead the way," I urged with a grin.

So Greg led me to a modest room that held a table and several chairs. There was also a large box with a window on the front that stood atop a tall, wheeled cart. When the Captain worked a button on the box, a dull light filled the window. Then he knelt before a smaller, black box on a shelf below the larger one. After touching two buttons on that device, he joined me in sitting at the table as we faced the windowed box.

"This is what we call television. It's the medium that Anita works through to bring her news stories to the public."

I nodded and was about to say something when a somewhat slender, notably cordial gentleman appeared in the window and announced, "What you are about to see may seem like the elaborate prop for a motion picture, but I can assure you it is not. Our reporter on the scene is Anita Blake. Anita."

With that, the man disappeared and was briefly replaced by the young woman in question who said into her stick, "Peter, what you are about to see still amazes me. Yet, I have to emphasize that it is real—*very* real!"

As the picture changed to an aerial view of *Scorpion* lying at anchor after her encounter with the pirate, Anita continued, "This is the bark *Scorpion*, a United States privateer, shortly after her latest engagement earlier this afternoon. My crew and I were en route to doing a vacation story when we intercepted a message from the Bahamian authorities asking the U.S. Navy to intervene on their behalf. We went to investigate and found *Scorpion* waiting for the arrival of the American frigate *John Paul Jones*. It appears that *Scorpion* unknowingly chased a pirate ship named *Graywolf* through a time warp from the year...*1777*, defeated the pirate, rescued a woman who had been abducted by the pirates, and then sank *Graywolf*. The following is part of a video tape we obtained from a vacationer that shows the two ships doing battle."

I was, of course, startled by what I saw. Here was *Scorpion*, guns booming, with our second broadside. The pirate gave her ragged reply, further enshrouding us in white smoke. I even heard myself giving orders to prepare for boarding. At the same time, I felt a proper degree of pride as I saw my ship swing alongside *Graywolf*. Then Anita returned to explain that we went on to board the pirate, before the view changed to one of her conferring with several people on the beach.

SCORPION—James R. Poyner

Finally, she added, "I would have found this story just as unbelievable, Peter, except that I managed to talk to several other vacationers who witnessed the entire episode. Further, as this scene shows, you can see a sailing ship lying below the water with debris still swirling about where it went down."

"Well, I'm convinced, Anita. Did you get to talk to anyone on *Scorpion*?"

"Yes, I did. This next scene shows the bark entering the harbor at Nassau and being greeted by a flotilla of small boats. Now here I am going aboard."

We then watched Anita's brief interview with Tibbs and myself, followed by her short tour of the ship. When Peter thanked her and went onto something else, Greg got up and shut off the television and other machine. At first, I didn't know what to say, mainly because I was so amazed by what I had seen.

"When did others see this?" I finally asked.

"Yesterday evening. You made nearly every paper this morning. To me, all of that is good. It means the Navy and the government can't pretend you're a figment of someone's imagination. They have to accept your presence among us, and that means they have to make room for you. How this will affect the Board of Inquiry, I couldn't say. At best, it reinforces the idea that you were operating according to procedures of your time. Still, I thought you should see that, not only to put you on equal footing with everyone else, but also to introduce you to television and show you how many Americans get their news these days."

"Well, now I can understand what the Bahamian Captain meant when we first saw the ABC helicopter. That is, he said..."

Just then, one of the Captain's men knocked on the door and cried, "Captain Brosky!—urgent message from Comfleet, sir!"

After briefly studying the sheet of paper, *John Paul Jones*'s commander frowned and said, "Well, Sam, we—your ship and mine—have been assigned to handle an incident off the coast of

SCORPION—James R. Poyner

Cuba. Seems that one of their gunboats is holding *Southwind*, an American cruise ship, for violating Cuban territorial waters without permission. Castro—he's the president of Cuba—wants a billion dollars from the company that operates *Southwind*, and if he doesn't get it in three days, he's going to order the gunboat to sink *Southwind*."

"Why, this Castro sounds like a modern *pirate*—holding people hostage, while threatening their lives if they don't obey and yield to his avarice! How can Cubans allow themselves to be ruled by such a man?"

"Well, he's something of a tyrant. I guess the majority of Cubans are either afraid of him or they still regard him as a hero from the days when he came to power. Yet, you're right this business reduces him to nothing more than a pirate." Greg glanced through the dispatch again and sighed, "Unfortunately, Comfleet's orders are kind of vague. We're to go there and try to *ease* the situation— whatever that means. I guess they're hoping that we can simply scare off the gunboat. Here's an aerial photo."

Naturally, I was fascinated by the photo, and then I noted, "You know, if we time our arrival carefully, Greg, we may be able to do just that—scare off the gunboat."

✳✳✳

LESS THAN AN hour later, still early in the afternoon, both ships were underway, sailing southeast. Duty had called us away from paradise. Obligation had risen and cast us into an abyss of uncertainty and danger. Yet, we went willingly because that was dictated by our allegiance and propriety. Our nation needed us, and that was enough. So we went at a pace that was steady and sure. Our confidence was high, thanks to a quickly formulated plan of action that called upon the best traits of *John Paul Jones* and *Scorpion*.

Miss Walton was now especially glad that she had taken a berth on *John Paul Jones*. She acknowledged that *Scorpion*, with its gun deck awash with the turmoil of battle, was no place for her. It was not that she was faint-of-heart, it was more that she was concerned about getting in the way of my crew as they were employed in our very serious task. With a smile, she hoped I would appreciate that realization. However, on another tact, Greg had asked her to join him in the bridge whenever she liked.

"I appreciate that and the consideration it comes from, Miss Walton," I noted as we stood near the top of the stairs to the launch, just prior to my departure. "I also appreciate the fact that Captain Brosky isn't the sort of man to go through life as a bachelor—mark my words!"

"He's *not* married?" she wondered with a revealing interest.

"Not only that, but he has hoped I'd put in a good word on his behalf with you. Of course, I will because I can. He's a good man, and it goes without saying that he's successful. He's also told me that he finds you most interesting. Should I, therefore, encourage him to find time to share with you?"

"Ohh, please do."

Greg was on his bridge, of course. His crewmembers had given us a respectful distance. They were no more certain of what we might say or do than we were. Yet, none of them wanted to interfere with whatever might transpire.

"Then I will. What is more," I continued, "I agree that it is more important for you to learn all you can about our new society. I've already learned much from my visit to this ship, and I intend to pass that knowledge onto my crew, while I sense that you are already well embarked," I added in a vague reference to her current garb, a long denim skirt, gray blouse and white canvas shoes.

"Ohh, I am glad to hear that you'll see to your crew, Captain Dawes. It was my hope that we first learn how to fit into our new society, before we learn anything more. Yet, I would feel quite ill at ease if gallant *Scorpion* and her brave crew were lost in that way."

I smiled and wondered, "Gallant and brave, hey? Why you make us sound like some sort of knight-errant. Fascinating. At the same time, it may prove best to do both concurrently—learn about our new society while trying to fit into it."

"Why, that is most sensible! I will keep that in mind, Captain," she answered. "Well, once again, thank you for saving me from Captain Barber's cruel intentions. Someday, I hope to return the favor."

"I appreciate that hope, Miss Walton," I admitted, touching my hat as I lightly bowed. With that, I added, "Well, I will leave you now. You're in capable hands here. Farewell for now."

"Farewell, Captain Dawes!" she wished, before I descended to the waiting launch.

Yet, as I first stood the bow, Greg came out of the bridge and looked at me as he called, "Well, Sam, what's the word?"

"The glass is *up*, Greg," I replied, making him smile with understanding at the coded message.

At length, our bark plied on with *John Paul Jones* a few hundred yards off our starboard bow. Night came on with its ebony fullness dotted by the ivory stars that made way for the Moon silently traversing the heavens. The nightly grandeur was inspiring, while the silence, which ruled above the ever-lapping waves, could have been overwhelming if we weren't among friends. Perhaps, that is the most important aspect of the bond between shipmates. Through that tie comes the willingness to share *every* challenge that visits the ship. Through our bond comes the want to defend the ship, each other, and all actions—past, present and future.

It was as night was showing signs of ebbing that *John Paul Jones* signaled, *Farewell!* and turned to starboard. As she went, the frigate adopted a course that would bring her to the scene of confrontation from the north. We continued southeast for just half an hour before we turned a hundred and thirty-five degrees to starboard, or due west.

Our solo southeasterly tract had brought more than its canvas-filling posture to us. It also brought a steady drone that seemed to come from above and a ways to the south. Then, when we swung to the west, the drone seemed to become more pronounced. Yet, my need to concentrate on the ship kept me from looking through the southern quadrant for the source of the noise. Danger lay ahead, not over my left shoulder. Further, at that moment, I was at the starboard rail, while the droning was to port, which meant any attempt to search for the noise would be blocked by the sails. It may also have been that I had a sense of what the droning was, which in turn suggested that it was harmless.

By then, the sky at our backs was tinged with a rosy pink. It was unfortunate that we could not fully appreciate Aurora's awakening that morning since the eastern sky was laden with the promise of a spectacular sunrise. Had we been less experienced and less able to concentrate our energies on accomplishing our most serious task, I have no doubt that we would have succumbed to the inherent beauty of dawn's goddess. Instead, we held to our course while I sent the crews into general quarters. Although our intent was still based on chasing away the gunboat, we had to be ready for any turn to the worse. There is no point in creating a confrontation if you are unprepared to meet all of its possible outcomes, and for *Scorpion*, being prepared meant manning and arming all of our pieces, something that had to be done if we hoped to counter the swiftness of a modern ship, both in maneuverability and firepower.

As we continued in that direction and I watched the gun crews preparing their pieces at a good, mistake-free pace, I urged them to remember their earlier instructions. That briefing had been centered on a prepared illustration of a Cuban gunboat that Captain Brosky had brought over from *John Paul Jones*. With Greg's help, I had pointed out the key features of our opponent.

The gunboat was armed with two 3-inch guns and two fifty-caliber machine guns. The former were mounted fore and aft of the central cabin, were not enshrouded in steel, and could be pivoted some three hundred degrees, stops being placed to keep the gunners from turning too far and bringing their weapons to bear on the cabin. Captain Brosky had then described the machine guns in good detail. Essentially, they were muskets that fired rounds in rapid succession, and they were mounted to each aft corner of the railing enclosing the main cabin's upper deck. Their primary use was to shoot down aerial opponents, although they could also be trained to strafe the deck of a belligerent ship that got too close. The four guns were to be our main targets if we went into action. The other main features of the gunboat were its central cabin as well as the pilothouse, funnel and longboat topping it. All of those were considered secondary targets.

While I paced and watched my men preparing for battle, I naturally hoped that a fight wouldn't be necessary to end the situation that lay ahead. No warrior, no matter how seasoned and efficient, likes war. If for no other reason, we prefer peace and harmony because we want to avoid the fear that can initially visit every fighter in every battle. Yet, it is the role of our profession to be ever ready to go into battle when it becomes a matter of challenging evil, aggression, and injustice, and to only claim victory when we have restored the peace and harmony we prefer.

So we drill and train to maintain our sharpness, even though courage, the most important thing for any warrior to maintain, can't be taught. Instead, we *learn* how to call upon it each time we anticipate the need to go into battle. Unfortunately, courage can quickly vanish, or be impossible to summon, if a warrior feels abandoned by his country or his cause. That is the danger in looking on such warriors as some sort of necessary evil. In America, those warriors want to do what is right. They want to uphold justice and right, freedom and dignity, while challenging true evil with their very lives.

For my crew and myself, it was readily clear to each of us how the United States lauded *Scorpion*'s bravery in 1777. Had we returned to our Boston with Miss Walton and the treasure chest, our feats would be duly noted and honored. We would be considered heroes of our young nation. We would be encouraged to keep up the good work. We might even receive a commendation from Congress. In 1777, people knew how to say thank you to their brave-hearts.

But how did such feelings and regard for military heroes fair in the modern world? Were the cheers at Nassau an exception, or were they typical? Would our modern naval superiors laud us as well, or scoff at us for being crude and barbaric?

Yet, until we learned otherwise, we *had* to assume the nation's attitude was unchanged. We had to draw on the pleasant memories of our welcome at Nassau. For me, that assumption of continuity was a perpetual hope since I shuddered to imagine myself being part of a nation that could no longer stand up to the bullies of the world because it had plucked the hearts of courage from those who had chosen to defend it.

In the meantime, the sharpness my men displayed, as they prepared for our possible battle with the gunboat, reminded me of how Captain Whyte had often urged, *Learn your accuracy first, lads, and the speed will come. It's no good to misload because you were hasty. Not only could that be dangerous to you and those around you, but it also means that your gun has no chance of hitting its target, and that can be fatal to the entire ship! Yet, even if you properly load your piece, a hasty aim can still make it miss. So, remember, accuracy always comes ahead of speed!*

By the time Tibbs and his musketeers had received their instructions, which were to target the Cuban gunners, and they had climbed up to their posts, I had outlined our intended turns and so forth to Mr. Jenkins who stood the helm that morning. The other Mates were in the bow where they could help direct our movements while watching the actions of the gunboat. In the meantime, those not aloft or assigned to a gun were carrying out a variety of tasks. Some were still bringing shot and powder up from the magazine. Others were readying grappling hooks, planks and picks for a possible boarding party. One of the mess tables had been scrubbed with boiling water and covered with linen to receive the first wounded man who needed immediate attention. Yet, the eddy of commotion from going into general quarters was abating. Men were taking their final places, so they could act out their roles in the impromptu drama that lay ahead.

Then all was as it should be, and as always, a stilling tension hung over the crew and myself. A storm was about to break—one of *human* making. Soon the natural creaking of the ship, which we could hear so well at that moment of stillness, could be utterly *lost* in the boom and clamor of a sea battle. It all depended on those manning the gunboat.

If the calculated intervention of *John Paul Jones* and *Scorpion* failed to make the Cubans abandon their quarry, then a fight seemed inevitable, and so, when the gun crews announced their readiness, we were indeed prepared to confront the gunboat.

✳✳✳

NOT LONG AFTER our readiness was confirmed, Tibbs cried, "Ships ahoy!—two ships, five points off the port bow!"

Like many of my men, I took a deep breath with that cry. Danger, if it was to issue forth, was imminent. Death or life-long maiming could easily come from it. *Scorpion* could readily be destroyed if she was at too much of a disadvantage with our opponent. Then our place in our new society would be obliterated, while we were dispatched to a watery grave. Yet, such thoughts only briefly bobbed to the surface, before they were pushed under by our experience and by our courage that together elevated our confidence in what we were doing.

"Take us that way, Mr. Jenkins, and remember your turn, should we fire a salvo."

"Aye, sir!" he answered as we swung to west-southwest.

"Mr. Newton, standby to fire a warning shot."

"Aye, sir!" he returned as he stood near the starboard bow pivot gun.

A few minutes later, with the sun beginning to rise behind us, we came upon the scene of tension. The gunboat was a small gray ship, barely a hundred feet in length. In sharp contrast, *Southwind* was a towering mountain of white that looked almost golden as it reflected the first rays of the sun. They were indeed utter contrasts in a variety of ways, not the least of which was their size, coloring and what they represented. Yet, in this arena, David held Goliath hostage and threatened the peace.

The liner, which was several times longer, was pointed west as it held to its forced anchorage, while the Cuban faced toward us, toward the sunrise, as it rode at anchor some three hundred yards off *Southwind*'s port stern. They were exactly as Comfleet's aerial reconnaissance photograph had shown—no surprises or changes there. I was glad of that since much of our plan had been built around that picture, while it had been made flexible enough to allow for either or both ships to be swung about their anchor cables by changes in the current. However, the need for that flexibility evaporated, as the flow of water had moved neither ship.

As we steadily, almost silently approached the gunboat to angle across its bow, I noted a handful of her crew chatting and stretching as they stood about their port rail and kept a lax eye on the liner. Two more were in a similar posture of manning the forward gun, while not really manning it, as they hung over the same rail.

That gun, like its aft counterpart, was presently turned toward the cruise ship. Given the ships' relative positions and the general aim of their guns, it appeared that the Cubans had gotten their prey to yield by threatening her rudder and propellers, and that they were employing the same threat to hold her at bay. We were well within range of the gunboat when a man suddenly tumbled out of its bridge. Frantically, he cried to the others, while pointing and looking our way. As his crew looked, the sun's first rays momentarily blinded all of them, and I took that as my cue.

"Starboard pivot gun!—fire!" I cried.

The boom of that small cannon, while also sending a signal, shattered the stillness prevailing over *Scorpion,* as well as the general quiet of the early morning. The storm had begun. Would that disruption be brief and inconsequential? Or would it rage on, with clouds of acrid smoke filling the air while charges of fiery lead knifed through the billows after thunderous booms, until, like a storm of Nature, it had utterly spent itself? The boom made all of the visible Cubans look our way and point with frantic terror, horror that remained even when the shot harmlessly fell in the water. Interestingly, passengers on the liner suddenly appeared at its rails and quickly urged others to join them. I wondered if any or all of our viewers believed in ghosts although I thought I heard *Scorpion* in the urgings of those on the liner, while that was met with excited, hopeful cries and even some cheers. Otherwise, a few of the Cubans seemed to pause and wonder if their lazy stupor had cast them into some sort of wild dream.

Then I told my men, "Starboard gunners!—take your aim! Port gunners!—stand ready and watch your backs!" Using my trumpet and best Spanish, I informed the gunboat, "We are *USS Scorpion!* You have five minutes to leave these waters, or we *will* fire!"

As I finished, my eyes carefully studied the Cubans for a response, particularly the Captain of their ship. We had to be ready to respond to the least provocation. It was hoped that quick action would remove our disadvantage. If not, Greg would have quite a story to tell his grandchildren on a Winter's day.

In response to my words, the same officer began gesturing wildly at us as he shouted in Spanish. Their forward gun crew responded by turning their piece toward us, away from the liner. Just then, the great, deep air horn of *John Paul Jones* sounded and was answered by *Southwind*'s. We all looked to see the frigate come swinging around the bow of the cruise ship, as it came on the scene from the north. Greg had correctly guessed that *Southwind* would shield his ship from the eyes and radar of the gunboat, and allow him to play out his part without challenge. Before the Cubans could respond in any way, the frigate had sliced between them and the liner. Many people on *Southwind* cheered the action, but when my glass showed the Cuban Captain turning red, I urged my crew to remain ready. When he shouted at his men to fire, I gave a like command to our starboard gunners. It was just as I did that I again noticed the droning noise.

Flame leapt out of the Cuban bow gun and was rapidly followed by smoke and a three-inch shell. It made a sizable hole in the lower sail of our mainmast, narrowly skimmed over our ducking portside crews, and rained water down on them as it crashed into the sea. In the meantime, *Scorpion* was typically rolled to port as her starboard guns fired in near-unison. Overhead, our dozen muskets chattered, adding their own glimmers as cannon muzzles flashed in anger, disgorging the dozen twelve-inch balls of iron, spewing as many pungent clouds of white smoke, like an angered dragon. As those ghosts of burned black powder danced over the water between us, two rounds slammed into the forward deck gun of the Cuban, killing its crew and twisting its barrel, while others smashed the pilothouse and the anchor winch, severing their cable. Despite that, the machine gunner on the gunboat's near side readied his weapon and began to swing it our way. It was almost trained on me, when the man recoiled backward, blood soiling his shirt. One of our muskets had gotten him. As I glanced aloft, Tibbs merely touched his brow to me.

"Thank you, lad!" I called.

Then, at my command, Lieutenant Jenkins took us to starboard and steered to bring our port guns to bear on their port side. The move would also put us between *Southwind* and the Cubans, and I hoped it would further convince them to withdraw without returning fire, before I gave voice to that hope as I again urged the Cubans to leave, while I stood at our port rail. When their Captain ran back to the port machine gun and began swinging it our way, as he hotly shouted for their aft gun to fire, I commanded our port guns to fire.

Both ships reeled from that blast. Ours came from the recoil of our port cannon. The gunboat, on the other hand, seemed to react as though a powerful fist had hit it. The blow nearly lifted it out of the water, and when the smoke cleared, we saw that its funnel had been knocked over, while its aft deck gun had been reduced to a mangled pile of blackened metal, and its commander had become a bloody heap lying atop the ruined port machine gun.

When the surviving Cubans rushed out on the main deck with their hands up, I called through my trumpet in their tongue, "I say again, you have five minutes to *leave* these waters!"

"*Si, si!*" they responded repeatedly as they got their wounded vessel to hurry from the scene.

With that, cheers, erupting behind me, made me look to see the decks of the other American ships, lined with jubilant people gaily applauding our decisive restoration of order, and when my own men joined in with their own adulation, I strode over to starboard, took off my hat, and waved it in a joyful salute—peace and harmony had been restored, if only to that small part of the world.

⌘⌘⌘

Chapter X

ABLE

NOT LONG AFTER the sorely wounded Cuban had vacated the waters, in the wake of the sharp demonstration of our willingness, and as the boisterous tribute to our heroics began to elapse, the Captain of *Southwind*, his red and white speaking trumpet at his side, exited his expansive bridge, stepped over to the nearest railing, spied me, and touched the brim of his hat. I returned the salute of the heavy-set, older man who, like his ship, was flawlessly dressed in white. Without question, I welcomed the outward display of gratitude from Captain Davis, his passengers, and his crew. All of them had been rescued from the Cubans by our courage, and that made us their instant heroes, while their appreciation was all the reward we would ever expect. Yet, the time was already coming when we would also need their assistance, and in a way that was equally hard to discern.

After exchanging names, Captain Davis said, "Well done, Sam. You have my compliments and my gratitude."

"Glad to help, Ron," I replied through my funnel. "You have quite an impressive ship. How many does she carry?"

"More than a thousand, to include a sizable crew."

SCORPION—*James R. Poyner*

"Bigger than some towns!" I noted, and we smiled.

"Captain," Mr. Newton said from my elbow, "Captain Brosky is signaling you."

Then, at the Second Mate's urging, I looked toward *John Paul Jones*. Greg was motioning to get my attention. After asking Captain Davis to excuse me, I strode the length of my ship and greeted Captain Brosky.

He brought his gray trumpet to his lips and told me, "Good shooting, Sam. Full ahead to Miami, with you off *Southwind*'s port stern! Got that?"

"I have it, Greg!" He had pointed out *Southwind*'s homeport on a map, and so, I added, "If we lag too much for you, leave us behind, and we'll get to Miami at our best speed."

"Understood!" he answered. "Do you have anyone needing medical attention?"

"None."

"Outstanding!" he thrilled. "Okay, we're getting underway. I'll stop by, once I get things squared away over here."

"I already look forward to your visit," I answered and issued orders for us to follow them north.

So, we swung about and joined our modern counterparts in heading north-northwest. *Southwind*'s massive engines pulled her a few hundred yards ahead of us, and then they slowed to let us keep pace. It was hardly necessary thanks to the good southwesterly that had come up to fill our sheets. With that, we sailed through the day of blue azure and easy seas, while up ahead many people gathered about the various stern rails of *Southwind* to watch *Scorpion* plying her element with a wonderful grace. Less than two hours after we had started north, *John Paul Jones*'s launch pulled alongside, and I welcomed her captain with a handshake.

"No formal welcome this time, Greg. My crew is too well-dispersed when we're underway," I told him. "Some are below decks resting after our long night, some, like Tibbs, are aloft as they always are during a sail, and the rest are seeing to clean-up details and repairs, to include the two sewing a patch to our royal main where the Cuban shell went through it."

"Huh?" he cried and followed my gesture.

Sure enough, hanging down either side of our largest piece of canvas were two of my lads. Each sat upon his own board that was hung like a playground swing from the royal yardarm. They worked by passing a large needle back and forth through the sail, steadily binding the patch of canvas to the larger, unfurled sheet. By then, they were more than half done and already singing a lively tune, with their mates in the rigging joining in when they could.

Realizing the task might need some explanation, I said, "That's the quickest way to repair a sail while at sea. The other way is to have several lads bring up the spare that we keep in the hold, and then we replace the damaged sail. Well, that's a lot of work, especially for a hole that's easily patched. So, once I determined that a patch would do, I gave Murphy and Piper the task. A bit risky, but there's no efficiency in the other way when the tear is so minor."

"Interesting. So, do you use those seats to paint the sides of the ship and wash the stern windows?"

"We do. Then the lads tie off on a railing and over they go. How about you?"

"We do something similar, but we have winches that employ small motors to hold the seat in place and raise or lower it." Then he wondered, "Well, is that the only hit you took during the whole fight?"

"Thankfully, it is. *Scorpion* doesn't mind a tear or two in her cloth, but how many of us can say that?"

"How true," he agreed with a nod.

Then, after a pause, Greg explained, "Well, I came by to tell you that the Board of Inquiry in Norfolk will include this matter as well. Comfleet just confirmed that. They also just told me that they aren't too happy about you shooting up the gunboat. I guess that's not what they had in mind when they ordered us to *ease* the situation. But what else could you do? They *did* fire at you."

Of course, Comfleet's concern puzzled me. I wondered what the Navy expected us to do when fired upon. Could it be that it was no longer fair to defend one's ship? Was that the way of *this* American Navy, prompted by the state of the times? Had we become so cautious and afraid of war that we were too timid to defend ourselves? I sincerely hoped that was not the case. Then I wondered whether Comfleet had even considered that we might meet with hostile fire. If so, what did they expect us to do when they sent us into the situation? Certainly, *Scorpion* wasn't built to withstand the sort of rounds the gunboat could fire.

"Why would they respond in that way?" I finally asked.

"Because it looks bad for the United States to be beating up on a little guy like Cuba," Greg said. "*We* look like a bully, and we lose credibility with the other small nations."

"Oh?" I mused. Then I offered, "Well, I fail to see how that could happen if the other nations are made up of rational men and women who recognize that the true bully in this is Cuba for holding *Southwind* hostage. Certainly, if Anita Blake from ABC had been there with her helicopter and Bill with his camera, there would be no question that we were in the right, that we fought because we were defending ourselves."

"True enough. Well, we got also enough witnesses on *Southwind* to verify our side, I say *we* because you won't be alone on this one. Since I was the senior officer for the operation, I'll be held accountable for our actions. I just thought it would be fair to warn you, Sam."

"I appreciate that, Greg." Then, after noting how he was a bit concerned, I consoled, "Well, we'll weather this storm as surely as we weather those of Nature. Of course, that assumes that the Board is made up of people of reason and courage, meaning those who have gone to sea, and fought man and Nature, at need. If not, then pray to God to send an angel of mercy to stand with us before the board."

Captain Brosky sighed and admitted, "That may be just what we need, Sam."

Seeing him still somewhat depressed, I gave him a detailed account of the storm that *Graywolf* had led us through, and then I asked, "Have you ever known such a fearsome spectacle?"

"I've been through a few storms—nothing as violent as yours. But, like you, we rode them out, and we're better for the experience. It's not hard to feel proud of yourself."

"Well, then why can't we ride out *this* storm that is merely of human making?" I asked, making him smile and nod with understanding.

"You know, Sam, I think we will," he agreed with a smile. "In fact, I think there's a way my ship can help," he added, before he pulled out a small, black, oblong device and spoke into it.

By then, I was too used to the premise of being steadily exposed to the wealth of technology in our new present, and I was no longer very surprised by any of it.

✳✳✳

UR ARRIVAL AT Miami was celebrated by an impressive flotilla of small boats that was many times greater than the one at Nassau. Consequently, it was even louder. A few boats even had signs, held aloft or fastened to their sides, that read: *LOVE YOUR STING, SCORPION! WAY TO GO, SCORPION! THANKS, SCORPION! WELCOME HOME, SCORPION!* From them, the crew and I at last realized that those signs and the loud jubilation were the current way of honoring bravery. At least, they were for the civilians. I still had my reservations about what the Navy would offer us, especially if it was so ready to condemn our recent actions.

After several minutes, we tied up behind *John Paul Jones* at the commercial pier that was owned by *Southwind*'s company. That white giant easily used up most of the other side of the same pier while it very nearly towered over everything, to include *Scorpion* and the single-level building that stood upon the pier. Yet, as we eased into our berth, a phalanx of sailors, dressed in sparkling white, marched through a wide door in the building. Their gleaming brass instruments and booming drums were nearly as lively as the tune they played.

"That's *Anchors Aweigh*, the Navy's official song. They want all of you to know that you're a part of the Navy. At least, they think you *should* be," Greg explained.

"Well, I *do* like the tune!" I agreed. "I'm sure Tibbs will want to learn any words attached to it. There are a dozen of them who like to sing in the evening."

"Sounds interesting. Sure, I'll see that he gets a copy."

Then Captain Brosky pointed down to the tall fence that blocked egress to the pier, and as I focused on the knot of people just beyond the fence, some armed with television cameras, two men opened the gate and waved those people inside, he observed, "Things like this always bring out throngs of people. Most simply want to catch a glimpse of newsmakers, a few collect autographs—signatures of famous people—and the rest...Well, the rest..."

"The rest appear to be news people. I can see Anita and Bill."

"Yeah, and she won't be the only reporter this time, Sam. I'll clear it with Comfleet and arrange a press conference. That's a gathering of reporters where one or more newsmakers make statements, answer questions or both. You should also remember your promise to Anita about an extensive interview and tour."

"Yes," I agreed, "this would be a good time and place for it. I see now where such a thing could also work to our advantage,

Greg. At least, it would be a good attempt to put us in a favorable light with the public, which might count for something with the Navy."

"Say, I like that idea, Sam!"

When the band stopped right before us, and its leader stepped forward, I called to him, "Well done!—my compliments!"

"Thank you, sir. Welcome home!" When my men, led by Tibbs, gave three cheers for the bandleader and his group, Lieutenant Mulford then asked, "Any requests, Captain Dawes?"

I asked for *Yankee Doodle Dandy*. Then, while the band played a lively version, my crew and I surprised them by singing along. As we did, passengers and crew from the other ships and those who had been waiting at the foot of pier came up behind the musicians. Responding to my waves of encouragement, many of those people joined in, while the various reporters and cameras recorded the soul-stirring occasion. If I didn't quite understand how communications and the media worked in our new present, I at least understood how to use them to our advantage.

As that tune ended and everyone cheered everyone else, Greg told me, "Well done, Sam! This is just the sort of exposure we needed to help our cause."

"That was my hope as well," I said with a nod.

"Good! As for the press and Anita, let me clear things with Comfleet, before we do anything."

"Go ahead. Perhaps, you can pause at the end of our gangplank and tell them as much."

"I'll do that, too," he said with a nod. Then he pointed into the crowd and observed, "Look, Captain Davis is coming this way. Let's see what he has to say before I go anywhere."

I agreed just as *Southwind*'s master reached the area below us. His smile was even broader, and I sensed that was due, in part, to some good news for us. By my command, our gangplank was lowered while I invited Ron to come on board. He was still thrilled at my invitation to board my ship as he stopped before me and saluted. Like Greg, he had a deep-seated appreciation for my ship, which was rooted in his heart as a sailor.

"Permission to come aboard, Captain," he asked nonetheless.

"Granted, Captain. This is Captain Greg Brosky of *John Paul Jones*."

"Ron Davis," he told Greg before he shook our hands.

When that was done, I asked, "Would you like a tour while Captain Brosky returns to *John Paul Jones* to communicate with Comfleet?"

"I would, but before you go, Greg, let me deliver my invitations for the two of you, your crews and Miss Walton to come over to *Southwind* for a celebration, beginning at six."

"That's a very generous offer, Captain," Greg said. "Let me clear that with Comfleet, as well. I should be back by the time you've seen Sam's ship."

That was indeed the case, and when he noted Tibbs standing nearby, Greg stepped over to him, and after they saluted, he held out a sheet of paper and said, "Tibbs, Captain Dawes thought you might like a copy of *Anchors Aweigh,* the Navy's song."

"He knows me well, sir. Indeed, I was hoping to somehow learn the tune, so me and the lads could try it. Thank you for taking the time to bring me a copy, sir."

"Least I can do, Tibbs," Greg added, before they exchanged parting salutes.

Then Captain Brosky stepped over to Ron and me, and reported, "Comfleet has no objections to us attending the party, but they nixed our having anything more to do with the press until after the Board of Inquiry, Sam."

"Board of Inquiry?" Captain Davis wondered.

"Yeah, it'll be held on this ship at Norfolk, and it will deal with Sam's fight with *Graywolf* and today's tangle with the gunboat. I got a feeling they mean to crucify Sam over the gunboat."

"Not if my company and I have anything to do with it," Captain Davis said firmly. "I'll talk to my boss and see if I can appear as a witness. I don't see why my company would mind since they have a lot of money tied up in *Southwind*."

"I would appreciate any help, gentlemen," I said. "Do what you can and will, but I will have *neither* of you sacrifice your career on my account. If this Navy can't tolerate a ship defending herself, then *I* no longer want to be a part of the Navy. That's my position, and both of you should understand that before you proceed any further."

With a smiling respect for my stated position, they agreed, and we talked on after Captain Davis sent an aide back to his ship, so preparations could be made for the gala, while only I noted Tibbs gathering his lads together near the bow.

✳✳✳

WITH SHORE PATROL detachments assigned to watch both *John Paul Jones* and *Scorpion*, nearly every man, woman, and officer from the two ships would be going to the party. Miss Walton would be attending as well, with Greg as her escort—he had followed up on my coded urging that he ask her. Everyone on *Scorpion* was going, while Captain Brosky had assured me that most of his personnel would attend. There were a half dozen who simply could not be allowed to go. Greg assured me, he would find a way to accommodate those people at a future date. His assurance was enough for me.

As for the treasure chest, it had been taken over to the great vault at Captain Davis's headquarters. There it would be held until its fate was decided—or ours. Otherwise, for both crews, brass buckles and buttons had been turned into veritable mirrors. We found and polished our finest footwear. Then we all donned our cleanest and best uniforms over our newly washed persons, before we assembled on the pier alongside each ship. By design, both groups then marched over to *Southwind*, with mine in the lead.

You may, of course, wonder why we would do such a thing. Couldn't all of us find our way to *Southwind*? Well, there is no better way to move a body of people than by marching them. Further, a carefully ordered phalanx can never be mistaken for a mob, even if it *runs* to its destination. What is more, marching means that everyone will arrive at the destination at the same time. Yet, there was more to conducting that march. Both Greg and I wished to remind our crewmembers that we expected them to conduct themselves in a proper manner. Toward that end, I had made it clear that excessive drinking would not be tolerated. We could not set a good example for anyone by being loud and disorderly.

I was, however, not surprised to find the many passengers from *Southwind* watching our approach. Certainly, people have nearly always enjoyed parades. Our viewers applauded our precision and then commented favorably as we climbed single file up the great gangplank. At Greg's insistence, I went first, stopping to salute Captain Davis and ask his permission for all of us to come on board.

"Granted, Captain Dawes! Stand here at my side. My crew will direct yours to the site of the feast."

"Very good, Captain." Then I noticed a familiar young woman standing beside him along with a just as familiar black-haired man, and after shaking hands with the latter, I greeted the woman with a slight bow and a tip of my hat, as I said, "Good evening, Anita. A pleasure to see you again."

"Why, thank you and good evening to you, Captain Sam."

"Anita is here as my guest because she is my niece," Ron explained, "*and* Bill is because he promised *not* to bring his camera! I hope you won't mind, Sam."

"Not at all," I assured them. By design, I had gotten Tibbs to tarry and asked, "Ron, this is my long time shipmate, Seaman John Tibbs. Tibbs, Captain Ron Davis of *Southwind.*"

"Honored, sir," Tibbs said, shaking Ron's hand. "Fine ship, Captain Davis."

"Thank you, John. You'll sit at the table with us, of course."

"Thank you, sir, but Tibbs'll do for me name. Never been too partial to John."

"Very good, Tibbs. I believe you know my niece Anita and her cameraman."

"Aye, I do. Good evening, Bill, Anita. Do you suppose I could go flying with you one time?"

"Why, of course. You too, Captain Sam," Anita added. "Tonight, though, I've gotten Uncle to arrange to let me sit next to you at dinner. I hope you won't mind."

"Not at all. I need to learn still more about your society—about *our* society—to include what passes for dinner manners. In fact, if Tibbs can sit on your other side, he'll learn as well, and then we both can pass that on to the others."

"Why, of course," the young woman replied with a fond smile.

Smiling, Captain Davis said, "Well, this should be a fascinating evening for all hands. You have much to learn, Sam and Tibbs, and my niece will be a good teacher."

"I'm sure she will be an excellent teacher, given her occupation," I noted, just as Greg brought Miss Walton up the ramp from the pier, the young lady clad in her newly cleaned pink gown.

They wound up on my other side at the great round table. Like Tibbs and the others from *Scorpion*, I learned much during the dinner and dance that followed. The food was excellent, as was the company. The music was very different from what we knew— although the orchestra did make a gallant attempt at Handel and Bach—and yet, it was also enjoyable.

As the orchestra took a break just then, Greg leaned toward us and asked, "So, Tibbs, have you had a chance to learn *Anchors Aweigh?*"

"Aye, sir, me and the lads meant to sing it when we marched back to our ships later on," my old friend replied.

"What's this, Tibbs?" Captain Davis wondered. "Do you mean that *Scorpion* has a ship's choir?"

"I like to think they're fairly good," I noted. "Oh, I know, Tibbs, you and the lads just do it for fun, but if you're up to it, this would be a splendid time to share your talents with others."

When everyone else encouraged Tibbs in a similar fashion, he wasted no time in gathering the choir on the modest stage. Then, after being warmly applauded for performing a couple of their sailing tunes, they surprised all of us with a lusty rendition of *Anchors Aweigh.* Greg was truly delighted by that, while Anita admitted to being at a loss for words. Yet, I also sensed from all of that that we would have little trouble fitting in with our new society.

All that remained, then, was the finding of the Board of Inquiry. Yet, I still saw it as little more than a storm. We could, with care and devotion, overcome it as surely as we did those of Nature. We could, with teamwork and strength, sail through its rough waters and get on with the rest of our life-long cruise. I felt we would succeed with the board, even if I didn't know exactly how that success would be accomplished. Ultimately, it *was* a test of faith.

So, like my men, I made the most of that night of celebration that was further enhanced as Anita and I steadily began to discover a mutual attraction for each other.

⌘ ⌘ ⌘

Chapter XI

SPIRIT

THE APPROACHING PALL of a Board of Inquiry was something for any sailor to respect and appreciate. That is, as I suggested to Greg, he has to meet it in the same way he treats any natural storm that comes across his course. He has to be aware of its sudden fits of temper, he has to keep an eye out for jagged winds, and he has to meet it with honesty and integrity if he hopes to survive. Yet, as with all storms, a true sailor knows in his heart that he can count on his shipmates to help in every way they can. Like the other sharp encounters, it is a test of the ship's unity.

So, once again, the premise of working together rose to the surface, the surface that was already beginning to heave. After all, it was the reputation of the ship that was at stake. Finding a way to uphold her honor would let us uphold our own. Further, even though only Greg and I could be punished, every man on *Scorpion* knew that he would be stained as well, if one or both of us were found guilty. The warning flags had been raised for Captain Brosky and me. The weatherglass was down. We were sailing headlong into rough weather. Soon, we would be sliding down the back of a great wave of turmoil into the foaming curl of relentless questions that impatiently waited to crash down on us, flinging their spray the length of the deck.

To face such a thing without concern was impossible. Yet, to deal courageously with that concern was in the power of every person willing to stand up to a bully. That's why I tried to ease Greg's concern from the onset, and in so doing, ease my own. Yet, I think he most appreciated the way my crew rallied around us, to say nothing of the support from his own ship.

That easement of concern was brought about in two other ways. First, Captain Davis's tribute, and that of his passengers and crew, had encouraged us to believe that we had done nothing wrong. Second, Anita assured both of us that *Scorpion*'s story was too well received, and that that had to mean something.

Of course, thanks in part to my evening with Anita, my burgeoning interest in seeing more of modern America had grown with each mile logged en route to Norfolk. What was this United States like? The glimpses I had had—helicopters, *John Paul Jones*, *Southwind*, speedboats, television and its many devices, the pier in Miami and its celebration, and so forth—were still only drops in the wide expanse.

Would I recognize cities like Philadelphia, Boston, Charleston and New York? Would all of us be truly able to fit into our new society, or would we forever be freaks of a freak of Nature? So, by asking Greg about our new home, I distracted both of us from our concern for the Board of Inquiry. Most of my questions came the day after the party when Greg accepted my invitation for him to sail to Norfolk on *Scorpion*.

As he returned from sending the launch back to his ship, a sheath of papers under his arm, I said, "Well, come below. It's almost time for lunch, and my officers will be delighted to have you join us. Then later today, you and I will map out a strategy for the Board of Inquiry."

"Sounds like a good plan, Sam."

"And, if you'd like a bit of a challenge that will offer a reward, then I'll take you where I often go when I need to put things in proper perspective."

"Well, of course, I enjoy challenges, and knowing you, Sam, there will also be something of merit bound up in it. Okay, I'll accept."

"That's the spirit."

Then, as we started toward the hatch, he added, "You know, I can't get over how much I *love* this ship, even though I've known her such a short time. There's something about her—something magical. Do you feel it?"

"I think I know what you mean. It's a feeling that's been with me since I was a small lad. Well, when Father first brought me down to Portsmouth. My love affair with ships and the sea began then, was greatly furthered by our journey to America when I was 12, and will likely never end, certainly not while I command *Scorpion*. Is that what you mean?" I asked as we settled into our places at the table in my cabin.

"I don't know. Maybe that's it. Maybe this ship reinforces my own love of the sea. At the same time, there's a sense that *Scorpion* is somehow alive—much more than *John Paul Jones*."

"I think that comes from the different materials used to build them. Moistened wood, taut hemp and wind-blown canvas make sounds that make us imagine that the ship is alive. At the same time, some feel each sailing ship has a spirit of her own, and that that's why some, like *Scorpion*, turn and run better than others. Certainly, the superstitious nature of sailors has much to do with such feelings. For my part, I choose not to dismiss any of it."

"I can imagine. Why take chances, right?"

"Exactly! Of course, I have always supposed that one reason we take such good care of our ships is that we all believe that the ship will be offended and stop acting favorably if we treat her otherwise."

Captain Brosky smiled, and when my officers entered, he asked them about the spirit of *Scorpion*. They pretty much agreed with all that I had said. Then Joe brought in lunch and smiled when Greg asked him the same thing.

"Well, sir," Joe began, "if you think about it, the wood, the hemp and the canvas that make up this ship were all alive at one time. And now, they can't help but be watered and exposed to sunshine, the very things that made them grow when they was alive. I'm not saying those things came back to life—I'm just giving you reasons for them to seem alive or to, maybe, have a new sort of life."

"That's a most interesting view, Joe," Greg noted. "Certainly, I'll keep it in mind while I sail with you to Norfolk."

After thanking *John Paul Jones's* skipper, Joe shuffled back to his galley, the five of us held our first strategy meeting for the Board of Inquiry, and when the meal and meeting had concluded, I said, "Come along, Greg, time to put things in proper perspective."

"All set, Sam," he answered with a smile.

He followed me topside and forward to the port ratline of the foremast, where I paused and, out of consideration, asked, "Do I guess correctly that you've been aloft as a cadet?"

"It's been a few years, but I'm up to the challenge. Is that what you meant?"

"Then follow me," I replied before leading him up that ratline and then up the second. "Would you mind some company, Tibbs?" I asked, as I poked my head above the large board that fanned out above the second yardarm of the foremast.

"No, come ahead, Captain. Welcome, Captain Brosky," my old shipmate added, as he maintained his spot and touched his brow.

The nest was a narrow board pierced by the top spar of the foremast. You might also recall that there was a modest railing fronting the board. In addition, there was a pulley-topped line for raising a signal flag or pennant to the top of the mast. I showed

Greg how to go from the ratline to the board, before we sat on either side of Tibbs and emulated his posture. With his legs dangling over the edge of the board, he rested his elbows on the railing, using his hands to maintain a good grip on the railing. There was no real advantage in standing, but being the man on duty had earned him the right to have the mast at his back, so he could periodically lean against it. Further, since it was both awkward and hazardous to stand, he had maintained his seat throughout our visit.

Yet, the view before us was, of course, extraordinary, no matter what the time of day. Just then, the sea was a lightly rolling greenish blue, flecked with lace of white foam, and presently dotted by the white pyramid of *Southwind* and the gray slice of *John Paul Jones*. Then on our left hand, and a few miles distant, was the green ripple of land, the East Coast of America.

"This truly is the proper perspective, Sam," Greg told me, as he sat to Tibbs's left. "How can you look at this and see all the inherent beauty and wonder fanned out before you, and not see things as they should be?"

"Aye, sir," Tibbs said. "This is the place for that. Captain Dawes especially likes to join me when I first go aloft in the morning. Not only can you get the proper perspective, but seeing the dawn come over the sea always inspires you with a sense of hope and promise. That's why I expect both of you will join me in the morning."

And, indeed, we did.

✳✳✳

LATE THE NEXT afternoon, our perspective reinforced by Greg and me going aloft with Tibbs first thing that morning, we entered the James River, some ten miles south of Yorktown, and followed our companions in turning to port. Many small boats were there to greet us with toots of their horns, or waves and cheers from their riders. Again, many American flags and welcoming signs were in evidence, to include those on a small fleet of fishing boats. Yet, even with the fishermen, the greeting was not as large or boisterous as the one we had known in Miami. I really didn't mind that. I was simply glad for the newest display of welcome. It meant that welcome was widespread, and that was encouraging.

As we turned to enter the naval base, we were honored with horn blasts from a number of the gray warships, to include one immense behemoth that Greg told me was the battleship *Iowa,* the last of its kind, capable of hurling two-ton projectiles twenty miles but made ineffective by its own size, much like the towering men-of-war of my day. Somewhere nearby, a band struck up the snappy Navy tune, while many sailors gathered at the rails of their ships to watch us pass. When they stiffened and saluted, I properly returned the salute. At last, *John Paul Jones* led us to berths at a pier, with *Scorpion* tying up behind our frigate counterpart.

That time, initially, though, there were no crowds to greet my ship. Greg's ship, however, had a fair collection of spouses and children waiting to welcome home their loved ones. That the latter took a moment to point us out was most flattering indeed. By arrangement, we then opened our ship to the crew of *John Paul Jones* and their guests, which included a parade of thoroughly delighted children. A goodly number of all ages took advantage of the offer, and so, still more camaraderie was built, while that eased any discomfort we felt, knowing that their were *no* loved ones to greet us. Then, that evening, at Greg's request, Tibbs and I had dinner on *John Paul Jones,* which was followed by the three of us viewing much of the frigate.

The next morning, with my crew and myself assembled on the ship's main deck, three grim naval officers and a stoic seaman followed Greg and Miss Walton up the gangplank and exchanged salutes with me. The senior officer was Captain Robert Trillet, a large, burly man with gray hair and a roll in his legs that marked him as a longtime seafarer. Yet, his gray eyes no longer had the sparkle of adventure in them. Indeed, the furl in his brow and mouth suggested that he was a man angry about where he was and what he was doing. I correctly guessed that he had been judged no longer fit to command a ship and had been given the duty of inquirer when he refused to retire. He was, then, a man to be pitied as much as he was one to be feared. We could suffer from his anger. Yet, what if, as Greg had suggested at lunch the day before, Captain Trillet could be made to see things from our perspective?

The ever-reserved Seaman Donovan brought a gray box mounted on a stand that he would use to produce a log of the proceedings. As for the other board members, Captains Pyle and Clorwich were both younger and inclined to let Captain Trillet run the proceeding and ask the questions. I doubted that either man had been to sea since his cadet days, and I wondered how it had been decided that they should help determine the fate of men who were able veterans of the great waters of the world. No, there was something wrong in that, and that sense was aggravated by my opinion that Pyle and Clorwich were the type of men who tried to get the most out of something, while expending the least amount of energy to accomplish their goals. During the hearing, they did little to refute that theory although they also did nothing to challenge either Greg or myself. It seemed, therefore, that if we could get Captain Trillet to side with us, we would indeed be acquitted.

Only Captain Trillet bothered to shake my hand, and, as he did, I offered, "Would you like to inspect my crew, sir, or should we proceed to the matter at hand?"

Trillet glanced about, sniffing the air. A faint smile suggested that something pleased him about my ship. I was not foolish enough to interpret that as pleasure in me, but I did see it as a possible opening. I tucked that thought away and carefully awaited his response.

"Fine ship, Captain Dawes. I'll see her and your crew after we're done."

"Very good, sir."

✳✳✳

AFTER DISMISSING MY men, some had repairs to make, one had armed duty to perform, and the rest had been assigned duties aimed at cleaning much of the ship, I led the party down to my cabin. Three chairs had been arranged on the window side of the table, while others were arranged before the table, so that there was a fair amount of space for both Greg and me to stand before the Board. After bringing coffee for all of us, which included my three officers, Joe shut the door and bustled back to his galley. Tibbs, armed with his musket, had been posted outside the door and was under orders to let no one enter unless the concern was of a very grave nature, or unless they had something to contribute to the Board. Even then, Tibbs was to knock and ask Captain Trillet if he would see the newcomer.

Finally, with everyone seated, and his aide, Seaman Donovan, ready to serve as court reporter, Captain Trillet rapped the table with his gavel and pronounced, "This Board of Inquiry of the United States Navy is now in session. The purpose of this board is to evaluate separate incidents, three days hence and five days hence, and determine if Captain Gregory Brosky and/or Captain Samuel Dawes are guilty of insubordination for disobeying orders, and if so determined, this board will decide the appropriate punishment, up to and including, relieving one or both officers of their command and subjecting them to general court martial. How do you plead to these charges, Captain Brosky?"

"Not guilty, sir."

"Captain Dawes?"

"Not guilty, sir."

"Then let us proceed," he concluded before asking me to describe, among other things, our pursuit of, and the battle with, *Graywolf*.

A good hour had passed by the time Greg and I had concluded our descriptions of both the incident with the pirate and the one with the gunboat. Ever so gradually, Captain Trillet's attention shifted to me. He began to feel that I was primarily responsible, particularly for the results of the battle with the gunboat. Yet, why?—out of ignorance for their ways, or with a belligerent disregard for orders? The latter would make me alone culpable, while the former could absolve both of us. Yes, by then, Trillet had concluded that Greg's only fault was through the circumstance of having *Scorpion* attached to him, while he conducted his operation.

"Captain Dawes," Captain Trillet began, "would you describe yourself as what we call trigger-happy? That is, it appears that you fired your guns at the gunboat with the least provocation."

"No, sir, that term does not apply to myself or to my philosophy as commander of this warship. Like any man, I approach battle with great caution and trepidation. In the case of the gunboat, the Cuban did fire first, and we responded in kind."

"With a broadside, is that correct?"

"Yes, sir, a broadside."

"I guess what I'm trying to say, Captain, is don't you think firing twelve guns, all at once, was a bit extreme?"

"Sir, I was schooled to fight a naval battle in a certain way. If those methods no longer suit the United States Navy, I will be only too glad to resign. However, even if I am forced to take that step, I would like to have one thing made clear."

Captain Trillet straightened, as if he was recoiling from my remarks, before he bade, "Proceed."

"Sir, with all due respect, we were sent to rescue *Southwind* from her predicament, and we succeeded without harm to *Southwind*, and without losing either of our ships. That should be noted with proper distinction by this board, as should the fact that it is poor policy to not recognize all successful missions, and to not acknowledge the courage involved by their crews."

Again, Captain Trillet recoiled, almost like a ship taking a broadside, before he spat, "Recognition!—you're a proud man to want *that* from us!"

"Proud? Yes, I am *always* proud of my crew, my ship and our actions. What decent Captain wouldn't be after all we've done and been through in recent days? But even before then, I had reason to be proud of all three. Ever since she became a privateer, and even much of the time prior to that, *Scorpion* has always been a model of devotion, dedication, consideration, and unity, and so, she is all that is good and decent, and she is what I hope our nation and society *always* will be. I'm proud, too, of the United States we left behind. She wouldn't let any nation, big or small, intimidate her because she knew that we had as much right as *any* nation to defend ourselves, no matter *where* that defense took place, just so long as we were flying our *American* flag." Initially, Captain Trillet began to recoil, but then, it seemed, his reaction softened to consideration for my words, and so, I continued, "Indeed, every victory won made us more independent, while it also preserved the cause of freedom and justice for all that our nation was founded upon."

Captain Trillet raised his brows at that. I knew from that, that there was a patriot in him. There still was. Yet, he also seemed to be considering me in a new light. I had as much fight in me as did my ship. It was also typical that a ship, both vessel and crew, reflected the spirit of her commander. No, I would not be intimidated, nor would I back down. There was, after all, an inherent value in a man such as myself, especially if I could teach others to behave the same way. Or did the Navy and the United States no longer want such men? If so, I would follow through with my offer to resign.

I continued, "In fact, if we had returned to our Boston from rescuing Miss Walton from *Graywolf*, someone of note, Captain Turnwick or another, would have said, *Nice bit of work, lads. Now, take a rest before you head back out to sea to do some more.* That's what I mean by recognition, sir. Someone from the Navy or the government to acknowledge our efforts, to say nothing of *twice* facing the danger of battle, without question."

"Ohh, I see," he said with a nod. "Well, I'll grant that your ship has performed courageously in *both* incidents, as has *John Paul Jones* in the Cuban situation, and you did rescue several thousand civilians, in the bargain. That's commendable, too. However, that doesn't mean you acted *properly*, Captain Dawes, which is what we're here to determine," Captain Trillet observed. "This is a *different* world from the one you left behind. I think we can concede that what you did with *Graywolf* was done in accordance with the customs and mores of *your* time, *and* we can concede that you were acting as if you were indeed still in your own time.

"However," he regretfully sighed, as if he wished the whole business could be so neatly dismissed, "what you did with the Cuban gunboat was done in accordance with those *same* mores and customs, which are not necessarily the same as those of the *present* United States, *and* while you no longer were ignorant of your place in time."

"Oh, c'mon, now!" Greg cried. "With all due respect, sir, no one can be expected to adopt and practice the ways of a society just two days after coming to that society."

"I don't like your tone, Captain Brosky!" Captain Trillet warned. "If I were you, I'd show the same self-restraint that Captain Dawes should have shown toward the Cubans!"

"If this ship was also made of steel and also armed with three-inch guns, I might agree with you," Greg added calmly. "Consider that, and the fact that hitting an opponent with everything is the way this ship *has* to fight against *any* foe of our time, which really isn't any different than the way she's *always* fought. I know, because I used my ship's computer to look up *Scorpion*'s history from its present. Did you know that in just under one year this ship took *ten* prizes, to include *Seacastle* and *Bennett*?"

"What's that?" Captain Trillet asked with sharp interest.

"Aye, sir, those two ships limped into Boston on June 23rd, 1777, turned *themselves* over to American authorities, despite Captain Dawes's hope that they wouldn't, and reported on *Scorpion*'s intervention that drove off *Graywolf*. Why, Captain Trillet, if *Scorpion* had returned to *that* Boston with Miss Walton, and otherwise survived the war, then, certainly, *Scorpion* would've become as legendary as *Old Ironsides*."

"That's quite a legacy, all right," Captain Trillet admitted. "*Ten* prizes, hey? That's quite a record, all right," he added, eyeing me.

"It is, sir," Greg said, "but it also means that this is too damn good a ship, manned by too damn good a crew, and mastered by too damn good a Captain, to be torpedoed by its *own* navy and through that navy, its *own* government!"

Captain Trillet started to stammer, to roll back from taking a new broadside, and I knew I had to intercede in an effort to save Greg's career. His arguments were sound, his research on *Scorpion* was admirable, but it really was for *me* to defend my ship. I had to demonstrate that I still considered my actions proper. I had to reiterate what I had said about defending my ship, and about restoring peace and harmony. I had to build on the merits of my ship and crew.

Yet, we were interrupted, just then.

⌘⌘⌘

Chapter XII

ANGELS AMONG US

A S MUCH AS anything, interruptions tend to be a part of life. How many of you can accomplish your daily labor without experiencing one or more intrusions during the course of each day? Certainly, it is easy to become annoyed by such moments. If nothing else, they delay completing the current task and, in turn, the day's requirements, while our inherent industry favors carrying out each task as soon as possible. Yet, if we exercise patience, and if we look at those disruptions as being a part of life, as I suggest, then they become less of an annoyance, even when the motive for them is something petty or inconsequential. What's more, how often, if ever, have such disruptions actually *kept* you from completing those assignments?—once?—twice?—*none?* On the other hand, what of those times when they have become something worthwhile? That is, how often have those interruptions turned into help to ease your burden?

Yes, just then, a new voice called, "Captain Trillet!"

"What!" he whined, as if under attack from too many sides. Then, noticing my disapproving frown, just as he realized whom the speaker was, he said more cordially, "Is there something you have to add to this, Miss Walton?"

"There is, indeed," she answered, and in a tone that hinted at her disappointment with the tenor of the proceedings, if not Captain Trillet's regard for my ship and me, her heroes.

Before approaching the table, she paused to remove a fold of parchment that had been pinned inside her hat. It was then I remembered her regretful moans about her uncle. I also remembered how she had acted as if she had somehow let him down when she learned of his fate at Yorktown. It was as if she had some knowledge to convey to Lord Cornwallis that might have saved him from his historical embarrassment.

Yet, before any of us could learn what Miss Walton had to add to the proceeding, there was a knock on the outer door, and Captain Trillet called, "Yes!"

Tibbs looked in and said, "Sorry, Captain Trillet, but Captain Davis, Anita Blake, her cameraman Bill Dakota, and another gentleman have asked to be let in, so that they may testify and bring evidence before the Board."

"Let them enter, Seaman Tibbs," the Captain bade with a smile for my friend.

Like the rest of us, Captain Trillet wanted to hear all that could be heard. He was a fair man, and he seemed to have realized that I was an able commander. It was just that his thoughts were governed more by politics than by decency, more by impression than the search for justice. It was a difficult path to follow, and I correctly sensed that his spirit, the one that would always makes him a sailor at heart, was being summoned by the very spirit of my ship, which was urging him to help me, and which was embodied in Tibbs more than myself or any other crewman. As such, Captain Trillet found it hard to do anything that would somehow harm *Scorpion*.

As well, as Anita, her uncle, and Bill, there was a man in a dark suit, who was identified as Mr. Henry Shaw, an executive with Ron's company. What's more, that day, instead of his camera, Bill was armed with a small television that had a VCR built into its bottom, while Ron, in addition to his satchel, carried a small red device that had a few switches and an electrical outlet built into it. You call that device a generator, and I am told that this one worked off something called a battery. Once the television had been set on a small table with the generator below it and accommodating the plug, Bill stepped over to me and held something out to me. It was an old arrowhead.

"Here, Captain, this has always brought me good luck, maybe it'll do the same for you. I certainly hope so."

"Thank you, Bill. Your hope is also greatly appreciated," I returned, patting his shoulder.

"Anytime."

Captain Davis then explained, "Captain Trillet, I wish to appear as both a character witness on Captain Dawes's behalf, and as an eyewitness to his battle with the gunboat. In addition, I have stuffed into this satchel a few dozen of the several *thousand* wires and letters I received from passengers, citizens, and even a *Congressional* delegation, authorizing me to voice approval of Captain Dawes *and* his actions. Further, my niece, Anita Blake, has a video that she would also like to place as evidence in this hearing. Bill Dakota, her cameraman, is also willing to testify, and Mr. Shaw, as my company's attorney and one of its executives, has come in the capacity of the company's official spokesman and observer."

"Very well, Captain, Ms. Blake, Mr. Dakota, and Mr. Shaw. Make yourselves comfortable. Miss Walton was about to add to the proceedings," Captain Trillet explained. "Come ahead, Miss Walton."

As she handed the paper to Captain Trillet, Miss Walton explained, "I was on my way to America to deliver this to my uncle,

Lord Cornwallis, when I was taken by *Graywolf*. This is a plan for encircling Washington's army and forcing it to surrender, thereby ending the rebellion. Had I been returned to him in our own time, and after my rescue by *Scorpion*, I would never have delivered this. That is the least I could do for this brave ship. But I would not have stopped there. You see, if you turn the sheet over, you will find a plan for trapping and destroying this very ship!" When Captain Trillet's eyes widened, Miss Walton added, "Yes, what Captain Brosky reported about *Scorpion* had reached the Admiralty, as well, and they decided to include that plan. Yet, now when that same ship rescues several hundred from a *pirate* of your own time, you are more willing to *condemn Scorpion*, her noble crew, and her gallant commander than to reward them with recognition and appreciation. Well, I say *shame* on you!"

Again, Captain Trillet rolled back, before Miss Walton added, "Surely, if we so ignore our soldiers and sailors, the time may come when they will no longer want to stand up to the bullies and pirates of the world. They risk their lives doing that! And you alone, Captain, should be wise enough to recognize that *Scorpion* is no match for three-inch guns! Perhaps, if you had seen her engulfed in smoke and battle, as we did when we came around *Southwind,* you would never have been so *hesitant* in recognizing the great danger this ship sailed into *without* question."

Captain Trillet flushed in response while his comrades remained as impassive as ever. It was also clear that Miss Walton's remarks also spoke to the seaman in Captain Trillet. They reminded him what it took to command and serve, as well as the inherent danger in any confrontation. They dared to ask him to consider what he might have done had it been him. They also asked him to consider the sad plight of a nation that no longer had the courage to defend itself.

"Miss Walton," he said, after a moment, and with what seemed to be a forced calm, "perhaps, Captain Brosky is right that you and

Captain Dawes can't be fully assimilated into our society in a few days." She sighed at his failure to yield to her point, and then the Captain added, "That being the case, you probably can't imagine how the rest of the world views what *Scorpion* did to the gunboat. Havana made a point of distributing photos of the gunboat to the press. It looks like a whirlwind tore through her, not an 18th Century bark, armed with two dozen 12-pounders."

"I've seen those photos," Anita observed. "If it was up to me, I would caption them, *Cuba Gunboat Gets What It Deserves*, just like *Graywolf* did, Captain Trillet. There's really no difference between the two, is there?"

"Yes, I'll grant you that. They were both acting like pirates, and even today, Captain Dawes would have every right to sink a pirate on sight. The trouble is, the gunboat wasn't flying a Jolly Roger, it was flying a Cuban flag."

"And *we* were flying an *American* flag!" Captain Davis bellowed, as he jumped from his chair. "That *should* give Captain Dawes every right to do what he did! He was defending *our* country, Captain Trillet! Can't *you* see that?"

"Of course, *I* can!" Captain Trillet returned, turning scarlet. "Look, I'm not questioning Captain Dawes's patriotism. He's probably got more of that than anyone in this room, if not the whole *blasted* Navy! All I'm getting hung up on is whether he used excessive force when he tangled with the gunboat."

"Captain Trillet," I said calmly, "this ship was designed to fire broadsides. That is the way she fights. That is the way she defends herself. That is what *we* were doing. We *were* defending ourselves from an aggressor, not to mention defending *Southwind* by association. We don't have guns or missiles that can target a foe miles away, nor do we have one set of weapons for defense and another for offense. What's more, the nature of the operation called for one of our two ships to get in close to the Cuban and provide a diversion, while being prepared to fight at close quarters. Naturally, that task fell to us because of our extensive experience with fighting in such a way."

"Well, certainly, I'm not questioning your tactics," Captain Trillet noted. "That much I can commend."

"Then commend Captain Dawes," Greg said. "It was his plan."

"Yes, I can see that. I think that comes from his more extensive practical experience. So, what went wrong, Captain Dawes?"

To that I responded, "Well, sir, our intervention and our firing a warning shot with one of our pivot guns wasn't enough to chase the Cuban away. Remember, further, the Cuban responded to our warning shot by firing its bow gun at us and putting a hole through our royal main. Had that round been a few feet to one side, it would have hit our mainmast, which almost certainly would have knocked it down and put us in grave danger. We can't afford to hesitate against a foe like that, nor do our pieces respond with the immediacy of your modern guns. Do you see what I mean, Captain Trillet?"

"Of course," he said with a nod, as he noted how my calm had restored the calm of the others. "Trouble is, I'm an experienced naval officer, and I have a fair understanding of naval history. That's something you learn at Annapolis, at the academy. Unfortunately, most people in the world don't understand what you mean by *immediacy*. All they see is a photo of a mangled gunboat next to a photo of *Scorpion*—like this."

He tossed a copy of the *Chicago Sun-Times* on the table. Its bold headline read, *Scorpion's Mighty Sting!* Greg, Anita and Bill glanced at it as well, and all three smiled.

"Well, what do you think, Captain Dawes?" Captain Trillet asked with just a hint of a smile, almost as if part of him was proud of that bit of evidence.

"I think, sir, it may be a long time before any warship, particularly one from Cuba, even thinks of taking an American ship hostage. However, if you condemn my ship and myself for acting as we did, that time might be much shorter, if it doesn't evaporate al-together, because there is inherent in such a condemnation the danger that *any* nation will think it can do such a thing and not suf-fer for its actions. Do you want that?—does the United States?"

"Damn!—but you *are* good, Captain Dawes! Yes, that's a pretty good point, but again, I'm not sure how much of it the rest of the world would understand."

"Well," I began, "then try to help them understand this. When, after our initial broadside, the Cuban Captain ordered his stern gun to target us, and then he himself tried to shoot at us with one of their machine guns, I had no recourse but to command a new broadside. I was taught, Captain Trillet, that when you are engaged in a fight with another ship, you keep firing until the enemy either strikes his colors or until he shows no further interest in fighting. If that is no longer an acceptable method of processing a sea battle—of defending one's ship and country—then I will gladly resign, be-cause it is the only way this ship *can* defend herself...especially against steel ships that fire shells."

"No, I guess it is wrong to question your methods, Captain Dawes, or to ignore your disadvantage, even against the gunboat. As for your methods, they really aren't very different from those used today. Further, any reasonable mind can conclude that a wooden ship is mismatched against one of steel," Captain Trillet nodded. "It's just this damn *photo!* I mean, it looks...looks like the gunboat was...was..."

"Like it was *scalped,* sir," Bill said, making nearly everyone laugh.

"That's it *exactly!* I mean, this was a first class *hatchet* job, and that's the problem. That's where the doubt resides—where *my* doubt resides. No, what I need is something to show the world that you *weren't* the aggressor."

"That's where Bill and I come in," Anita noted.

"Well, I've seen all your reports for ABC, Ms. Blake, but I don't think they'll be much help here."

"Ohh, I'm not talking about those, Captain Trillet. No, Bill and I are the only ones to see the tape we have to offer as evidence, because we agreed that it was more important to sit on it and use it to help Captain Dawes than to air it. That is, *Scorpion* will be an ongoing story. The sort of thing that people will *want* to learn about for some while, especially if we can clear her and Captain Sam...uh..."

"Captain Sam?" Captain Trillet wondered.

Reddening, Ms. Blake admitted, "Okay, I like him, and that's kind of my pet name for him. But it's more than that, Captain Trillet. Captain Sam—Captain *Dawes*—is one of the most fascinating men I've ever met, and this ship...this ship...Well, there's something about *Scorpion* herself. She's alive. She has a heart, and that heart would break if anything ever happened to Captain Dawes. That's what I mean too."

"Interesting. But what's this about another tape?" Captain Trillet wondered, as I glanced at Anita, more intrigued by her words about *Scorpion*.

After smiling somewhat sheepishly back at me, she replied, "Well, what I have to show you, Captain Trillet, might make the *Sun-Times* photo pale in comparison. That is, I believe that my tape shows that *Scorpion* acted to defend herself and *Southwind* at all times. It also tends to show how much more disciplined and precise *Scorpion*'s crew is, which may also have something to do with how they overcame their disadvantage."

"Yeah, that *would* make a difference!" Captain Trillet mused. "All right, show your tape. Go ahead, Bill."

After working a switch on the generator, Bill then activated the television. When it had been turned for all of us to view, Bill worked the play button on the VCR. I am still enamored of these video recorders. Television is a wonderful medium for reporting and entertaining. It also has a great potential for being able to educate. Yet, to have a complementary machine like a VCR that allows one to observe again recent news, enjoy a favorite play, or the like, whenever the need or want arises, that is what makes it such a charming apparatus, in my mind. Further, my views on that device are not entirely colored by what happened that morning.

The tape began with Bill's camera showing *Scorpion* sailing west, the first light of day coloring her canvas, giving it a rosy hue. In the background, we heard Anita making note of the gunboat and *Southwind*. Bill, however, knew better than to forgo his view of my ship. Moments later, our starboard bow pivot gun boomed its warning. By then, the gunboat was in the picture, as well, and it was not hard to see the scramble by the Cubans to take action. We could also hear my repeated requests that they vacate the area. Captain Trillet smiled at that. Then the Cuban bow gunners fired at us, the roar of our broadside followed, and with that, we saw Mr. Jenkins maneuver the ship to bring our port guns to bear, and to continue to place ourselves between the Cuban and *Southwind*. Captain Trillet also took note of that, and of the way *John Paul Jones* had come upon the scene. Finally, he heard my next round of warnings, before he saw the Captain of our foe again act with belligerence toward us, prompting our second broadside. That, after that, I again told the Cubans to leave the area was enough for Captain Trillet.

"So only you and Bill have seen this, is that right, Ms. Blake?"

"That's it. Like I said, we thought it might be inappropriate until this hearing was concluded."

"Well, thank you for the consideration. Go ahead and air it, but see that the other networks get a copy." Then Captain Trillet explained, "In fact, I want every person in the *world* with a TV to see what really happened. Is that clear?"

"Yes, sir," she said with a smile of understanding.

"Good." Then, after taking a moment to confer with the other panelists, Captain Trillet commanded, "Captain Brosky!—Captain Dawes!—attention!" He paused long enough for us to assume the position, before he announced, "This board hereby finds *both* of you *not* guilty on all counts!" When my officers cheered, while the civilians applauded, the Captain smiled and added, "Captain Dawes, welcome home."

"Thank you, sir," I said, as I saluted.

✻✻✻

BEYOND DISCIPLINE, THERE is one valued lesson learned in a military setting that, at times, fails to be repeated in civilian circles. It is at the heart of the reason for saluting. Saluting a superior not only demonstrates respect for that individual, but it also teaches the one saluting how to respect everyone. Such widespread respect does much to make a military unit cohesive, and therefore, effective. There is no doubt in my mind that the same result would be obtained in society if the same lesson could be somehow taught to all members of society. Of course, rather than salute each other, a handshake would suffice.

Yet, notice how my formula for respect is universal. It does not simply flow from inferior to superior, superior to inferior, as the salute is returned, but in all directions, both to and from every individual. I believe the crew of *Scorpion,* as I have suggested, is a most adequate model of that. Therefore, the results achieved by us are a small-scale version of what could be achieved by the whole of humankind, to the great appreciation of our Maker, for universal respect would go a long way toward bringing about peace and harmony for all.

After Captain Trillet returned my salute, Miss Walton cleared her throat, and with a nod from him, she said, "I'm glad this has been worked out, Captain Trillet. As I said, I owe my life to Cap-

...iss Walton and Anita," Captain Trillet said, "I ... too."

...oung women had blushed and thanked them, I ...on to one of them and asked, "Captain Trillet, ...ita and Bill accompany us topside? I still owe ...v, and I think Bill would like to take his camera ... nest."

...g smile, Captain Trillet said, "No, that'll be

...mind, Captain. Sure, I want to do that."
...d.

... to that, as well, Captain Sam, thank you," she ...mile that was filled with appreciation for me, and ...uragement for any romantic interest I might have

***

...RE WAS something in Anita's eyes that sug- ...at the promised tour and interview fell short of ...nt expectations, and since I had an idea of what ...d, "Of course, Anita, I think it would also be pos- ...or you, Bill, and even your uncle to join us on the ..."

...any objection from Comfleet on that," Captain ...ey like to keep the press happy by accommodat-

...ept for Bill and myself," Anita delighted after a ...er appreciation for me soaring to new heights and ...omise of a romantic involvement between us. Af- ...d his part of that invitation, his niece continued, ...d be awfully discourteous of me to hog you while

tain Dawes, his crew, and this ship. The passengers and crew of *Southwind* have the same debt, only they must also include *John Paul Jones,* her captain, and her crew, and while all of us have gone to great lengths to acknowledge their actions, it would be poor policy for the Navy—*or* the government—of the United States, to find a way to condemn those actions."

"There is that," Trillet noted. "Then, too, Miss Walton, you're right that if we don't properly treat and respect our heroes, they'll lose their reason to exist, to say nothing of their want to take such risks. What's more, it might not hurt this Navy to have a Captain with the *guts* to stand up to bullies and pirates, wherever they are. You're definitely that Captain in my book, Captain Dawes."

"Well, then, perhaps, that's something we can teach your cadets," I offered. "I say *we,* since my crew is just as willing to stand up to such villains."

"I don't doubt it," Captain Trillet agreed. "Still, there is one thing I'd like to know, Ms. Blake."

"Yes?" she wondered.

"How did you and your cameraman just happen to be flying overhead, so you could make that tape?"

"Well," she began, with a blushing smile, "when *Scorpion* and *John Paul Jones* headed *south* from Nassau—*not* north toward Norfolk—we guessed that they were up to something. Then, not long after that, we got a news flash about *Southwind,* and figured that the two incidents might be related. Fortunately, my pilot Mitch Anderson knew enough about logistics to help us estimate when the two would reach *Southwind.* That the time coincided with sunrise convinced me that we were onto something. That is, it seemed like the most logical time to stage the encounter."

When Captain Trillet nodded with appreciation, she added, "So we worked things out with Mitch to arrive several minutes early. When we got there, we shadowed *Scorpion* since she doesn't have radar. Then, once the fight started, Captain Dawes and the others were too busy to notice us, while we used *Scorpion*'s sails to hide us from *John Paul Jones*."

"So that *was* the droning I heard when we turned west," I mused. "Well, there certainly was no harm done, Captain Trillet."

"Maybe," Captain Trillet said, "but let's keep it to ourselves as to how Ms. Blake got that tape."

"Yes, that would be best," I agreed.

"Now, Captain Dawes, you and your ship will no longer be under quarantine, but you will need to wait here until your new assignment is issued," Captain Trillet said.

He then stood, and with a grin full of respect for me, he again offered me his hand. That time, we enjoyed a firm, jubilant shake. He also let his grin come from his newfound pride in me. In that way, he reminded me of Captain Whyte. That is, I realized then that Captain Trillet would take us under his wing, and see that we were properly regarded and used. That Board of Inquiry had shown him as much, and so, I saw where that hearing had become an instrument for helping our modern society officially assimilate us. Yes, it was through that forum that that society—*your* society—began to understand—and *respect*—what we did and were. It was through that medium that we were officially accepted.

"Thank you, Captain Trillet," I said. "Now, sir, until those orders issue, *Scorpion* is at your disposal. Might I suggest a modest cruise with yourself and Captain Brosky as observers. It wouldn't have to take us far from this port, and we could use one of these portable electric devices to power a radio, should you think that would be necessary."

"You know, that would be a nice break from being a hearing officer. Let me see what Comfleet thinks," Captain Trillet answered as he grinned broadly.

I knew from that that I had been right in judging that he longed for the smell of the sea and the thrill of a voyage. As for his desperate search for a way to exonerate me, Miss Walton had likely

stirred a memory that no man can condemn felt better about himse had found the sunlight good weather that lay thy sailor would. Then, thoughts turned to rel crew.

"Well, if it's all right, "We'll *all* go, Captai get a good look at *Scorp*

"Very good, sir," I re

"I think you'll enjoy crews I've ever known," first observed them.

"Why, wasn't that ju wondered.

"It was, and while som were understandably fatig looming cloud that sometl dampen their morale," Cap

"Somehow, I'm not su *Scorpion*'s crew because of

"Ohh, see here, gentlen about all of that. My crew s all too well that by worki and respecting each othe comes our way. That's it. make your crew that cohesiv

"That's an interesting phil

"One I'll have to try." Th certainly right about Heaven

"If you mean M can agree with that

After the two recalled my obliga will you mind if A her a good intervie up to Tibbs's crow

With a knowi fine...Sam."

"Bill?" I asked

"You read my

"Anita?" I aske

"I'm agreeable answered with a s with hopeful enc in her.

ET, TH gested t her curr that was, I offere sible to arrange mentioned voyag

"Shouldn't b Trillet added. " ing them."

"Then I'll ac nod from him, furthering the p ter Ron accept

"As it is, it wo

my many colleagues wait on the pier. Like I said, this is a big story, Sam, and journalists generally try to *respect* each other's right to share in such a thing."

"How many reporters are out there?" Captain Trillet mused.

"Oh, I would say two or three dozen," Anita answered.

"Well, we'll hold a press conference on deck, all right, Sam?" Captain Trillet asked.

"Of course, Captain," I answered.

"That's good," Anita added. "What's more, I wouldn't be surprised if the President takes even more of an interest in the whole business, especially if a Congressional delegation already has. He'll probably want to meet you, Sam—maybe your whole crew."

"Well, I hope it will be *all* of us. It's never fair to single out one person, even if he, or she, *is* the leader. Every person under that leader deserves the same recognition, if only because each has played a part in making that leader successful. So, if it is the latter, we would be honored," I said with a grin. "Yes, I think that is just the sort of recognition my men most deserve, after all of this, and the kind I would most appreciate."

After they all smiled, Greg mused, "So, Sam, what about the treasure chest you took from *Graywolf*?"

"That's right, you did make note of that during your testimony," Captain Trillet nodded. "I imagine the loot in that box is worth quite a bit of money."

"Almost a hundred million," Mr. Shaw noted. "We had to have it appraised when it went into our vault for safekeeping."

"Well, we had guessed it would have some value, regardless of where in Time we are," I said. "I also pointed out to my crew last night that the modern United States does not have the same desperate need for such wealth that the one we left behind had. Still, Tibbs was quick to observe that that treasure would be tainted—blood money—and that we might even find it to be more of a curse than a blessing. That was enough for the rest of the crew. So, we *all* voted to turn the chest over to the United States government to use as it sees fit. Will you see to that, Mr. Shaw?"

"Of course, Captain," he said with a grin.

"Why, that is *just* what you said would happen, Captain Dawes!" Miss Walton cried.

"Interesting," Anita mused, with a favoring glance at me.

With a fatherly beam, Captain Trillet patted my shoulder and pronounced, "Yes, that's just what we'll do, Sam. Now, let's go see your crew."

"Right this way, sir!" I urged, as I had often done during my tenure under Captain Whyte.

Then, as we led everyone above, I was confident that, working together, my crew and I would successfully meet every challenge that Tibbs sighted from the forward nest, and so, we would live out our lives in dedication and devotion to each other and to our *new* nation, and with a prayer that the wind would *always* be at our backs!

The End

Biography

James R. Poyner

Since graduating from Millikin University, in 1976, James R. Poyner has experienced an interesting blend of editing, proofreading, manuscript preparation, and graphics production. Much of that time, of course, has seen the tremendous, technological explosion, which has so dramatically changed writing and publishing, and like others, Mr. Poyner has steadily adapted. At the same time, his professional experience has taught him how to mend and improve the written efforts of others, while further teaching him how to do the same with his own efforts.

Among others things, he has developed an excellent, self-critical inner ear. The smooth, fluid style of his prose is evidence of that. Add to that, the texture, rhythm and color acquired from writing verse, and the result is something <u>any</u> reader should appreciate and enjoy.

SCORPION, at first blush, is a sea adventure with a little science fiction thrown in. But, thanks to its themes about teamwork, respect, and its various contrasts, it is more than that. It is also one of his newer efforts, having been begun in the early 1990s.

⌘⌘⌘

ISBN 1553690265